Drover
and the
Designated Hitter

Books by Bill Granger

DROVER AND THE DESIGNATED HITTER

The Third Drover Novel

Bill Granger

William Morrow and Company, Inc.   New York

It is the policy of William Morrow and Company, Inc., and its imprints and affiliates, recognizing the importance of preserving what has been written, to print the books we publish on acid-free paper, and we exert our best efforts to that end.

Library of Congress Cataloging-in-Publication Data

Granger, Bill.
  Drover and the designated hitter : the third Drover novel / Bill Granger.—1st ed.
    p.   cm.
  ISBN 0-688-11884-4 (acid-free paper)
  1. Drover, Jimmy (Fictitious character)—Fiction.   2. Private investigators—Nevada—Las Vegas—Fiction.   3. Sports betting—Nevada—Las Vegas—Fiction.   4. Las Vegas (Nev.)—Fiction.
    I. Title.
PS3557.R256D765   1994
813'.54—dc20   93-43217
                                              CIP

Printed in the United States of America

First Edition

1 2 3 4 5 6 7 8 9 10

For Alec Granger, whose game is really b-ball anyway

PRINCIPAL CHARACTERS

Jimmy Drover—Ex-sportswriter who snoops for a Las Vegas bookie named Fox Vernon to uncover troubles in pro sports.

Black Kelly—The retired Chicago fireman who opened a saloon in Santa Cruz that was politically incorrect—and befriended Drover.

Homer White—The bigoted Arkansas power hitter in the middle of a long-term contract with the Cubs who hurts his legs in an off-season truck accident—and wants to be traded to the American League, where he can become a designated hitter.

Mae Tilson—Homer's vengeful ex-wife, who sells real estate in Seattle and sleeps with a man who sleeps with the mob.

Helen Brown—The thoughtful physical therapist in Chicago who restores Homer to painful health. Homer falls in love with her.

Eddie Briggs—The Cubs' general manager, who won't trade White but wants him to stay in the National League and keep suffering . . . because of something between them in the dark past.

"Let's play two today!"
　　　　　　　　—Ernie Banks of the Cubs

Hold On a Minute and Listen Up

This is the third story I've told about Drover and Kelly and the rest of them. You will see old faces in this story and some new ones. The thing to remember is that this is about sports and life and not in that order. So if you're not terribly interested in baseball (or in football, the first book, and college basketball, the second book), that's all right. Life is a lot more than just sports and gambling and hanging around a saloon in Santa Cruz or betting the odds in Las Vegas. The only thing you really have to know at the start of this story is that Drover is still a former sportswriter done wrong once by a U.S. attorney in L.A. who indicted him on phony charges. Well, one other thing. He is a sweet guy but he can never learn to say no or keep his mouth shut when he has the opportunity to say the wrong thing. OK. One last thing if you don't know anything about baseball: A designated hitter is a position in the American League where you hit in place of the weak-hitting pitcher. You don't have to run in the field or play defense or anything. You just got to hit the ball when they call your number.

Much like in life.

—Bill Granger

ONE

DROVER USUALLY went up to Seattle when he had to get away.

In this case, he was writing the "spring" book, so called because it was due at the publisher's office by April 15. It was an easy-to-remember deadline, coming as it did on tax day. Taxes were one reason he worked.

Drover had peace and sun in Santa Cruz, where he rented an apartment from his landlord and friend, Black Kelly. But he also had friends there. The trouble with writing a book on deadline was the gregarious nature of Kelly and of their mutual friends. People dropped in all the time at Kelly's saloon on the long pier in Santa Cruz. Kelly was a retired Chicago fire captain who had found a second life in the northern California town. The pier was abuzz with boutiques and seafood restaurants reflecting the fact that it was stuck in the Pacific Ocean. Kelly defied his surroundings with red-meat dishes, calorie-laden casseroles, and other examples of "Midwest Firehouse cooking." His several thousand friends ate there.

Seattle was different. Friends didn't drop in on Drover up here.

He rented a room in a no-name hotel downtown and settled in on the book.

Writing, when it goes good, is very good. When it doesn't go good, Drover likes to remind his Writer's Block that it beats working for a living. As a result, the books get done.

When he wasn't writing, he let the words escape out of his brain by wandering the rain-dazzled streets of the city. Day and night. It is a singular sort of city, full of loners and drifters and seamen trapped temporarily on land. The night is full of foghorns. The big ships cruise in and out and there is a melancholic damp over the sheds and piers and along the stalls of the Public Market on Puget Sound.

Drover didn't need company to be happy. He felt like the invisible man, spying on the world around him without people even knowing he was there. He had been that way when he was a kid, climbing on rooftops and lying in wait on the unsuspecting world below.

"Don'cha get lonely?" Kelly asked him once. He honestly never did. The world was full of other people and their plots and hopes and dark desires, and all Drover ever had to do was stop and spy on them to be part of it. Of course, he never told Kelly this because Kelly wanted another answer. Since Kelly was his friend, he got it; if you can't lie to your friend for his sake, then what kind of a friend do you call yourself?

Tap, tap, tap. The words would come to him and somehow make his fingers move across the keyboard of the Zenith laptop. Drover never thought about the process of writing, only the thought behind the words.

Sometimes at night he'd drop in to a bar full of strangers and join them. There was always some sports to talk about. It's the common glue used for male bonding in America.

The spring book was called *Fox Vernon's Pro Football Guide* and it came out every July and cost $9.95 on the newsstands. It was an honest rundown on the prospects of the twenty-eight teams in the National Football League, their relative strengths and weaknesses, and it peeled the skin back on some of the personalities crazy enough to play the game. The name Jimmy Drover was nowhere to be seen in the pages, though Fox Vernon wanted to share credit. Fox was the front man, a smart games-cruncher in Vegas who set lines and ran a sports book.

Drover had a network of football writers from every city with a pro team. He doled out $500 to each in return for their unvarnished look at the home team. They were guys who wrote one version for the paper and told the truth for Drover every spring. Thirty-one notebooks full of the truth and Drover just filtered it down to one coherent read. It felt good writing it, felt good not having his name on it. Just a kid playing spy lying on a rooftop somewhere, watching the world without being watched in return.

On this particular rainy night in April, the fog swirled in on the city from the Sound and a freighter going to Alaska blew a mournful horn of departure across the waters.

Drover walked down Alaska Way, thinking about things like the Bears' secondary and whether Washington would repeat and why the Indianapolis management system was so bad. He didn't even notice the car following behind him that was going as slow as he was.

The book would be finished in a couple of days and then he could go back to sunshine and Kelly's pot roast. He'd have to call Lori Gibbons because she had called him before he left Santa Cruz. They'd arrange a date and he'd maybe go down to Florida to see his old Chicago pals settled in Clearwater Beach. Back to life in a couple of days. The exile in Seattle was like a retreat. He felt like a new man.

The car was a fashionable deep-green Cadillac with blacked-out side windows. There were two men inside, both in the front seat.

Drover's hands were deep in his raincoat pockets and he was wearing an old fishing hat to keep the raindrops off his head. The rain was cold. He was beyond the Public Market now and in a sort of twilight zone of commercial buildings that led down to the Space Needle. Downtown was connected to the site of the old World's Fair with a monorail that reminded Drover of the El in his native Chicago.

It is a good neighborhood to be accosted in at this time of night, especially a rainy night.

The driver's-side window slid down with a whirr and the man behind the wheel stared at Drover. Drover stared back.

"You wanna ride? It's a crummy night to walk in," the driver said.

Drover came to the side of the car. "I've got a choice?"

"It's a free country."

"Really? I thought it cost like everything else."

"We wanna talk to you about somebody."

"Somebody I know?"

"Yeah."

"Then why not call my office for an appointment?"

That made him blink. "I didn't know you had one."

He knew the driver, of course, but not the other guy hidden in the shadows of the big car. The driver was no friend of his. But, as he thought about it, he probably wasn't on an enemy's errand either.

It didn't matter in any case. There was no question that he was going for a ride.

He opened the back door and got in. The second man wore a felt hat that put a shadow on his face.

The car purred ahead, picking up speed. The driver turned uptown, toward Fifth Avenue.

"A certain guy is deep into our pockets," the driver said. "I am talking about Sal Marconi's pockets." The driver worked for Sal Marconi. He was called Elmore by everyone in Vegas and he hated the nickname because it had taken him a long time to understand it. He was of average thickness in head and body and his skin was the color of slightly burned olive oil.

"You shouldn't give credit."

"This wasn't the casinos."

"Then I don't want to hear about it."

"You're getting picky, Drover."

"I'm not in your racket, Elmore. You've got a lot of people who know how to extract monies due. It's nothing to do with me. Sal has a problem, let Sal take care of it."

"But you're a sports writer."

"Was a sports writer."

"So you know sports writers. You know your way around."

"I know enough to not listen to you, Elmore. Or take candy from your friend there."

That stirred the second man. He turned to look at Drover in the back seat. The lights of the streetlamps passed them in and out of shadows.

"You know me?"

Drover stared at him. He hoped he was staring hard enough to impress the fat man. The guy had to weigh three hundred pounds and he had fat baby cheeks and tiny little eyes.

"I said, 'You know me?' " the fat man said.

"No, but I still wouldn't take candy from you."

"This is a funny boy," said the second man.

Elmore kept his eye on the road and his big paws on the wheel. The wheel looked small.

"Drover," Elmore said in his growly voice. "I was only filling you in. On the background, you might say. This guy owes big time to a couple of hard cases from Chi."

"I hate it when you say 'Chi,' Elmore. Just like they hate 'Frisco' in Frisco. City's got a name. Use it and stop getting your elocution lessons from Grumpy here."

"This is a funny boy," the second man said a second time. Something about the voice brought up the generally scuzzy feeling of *Key Largo*. Drover made a face and leaned toward the back of Elmore's head.

"Why are you and Grumpy here? In Seattle?"

"Because you are here," Elmore said.

"Maybe I'm in Seattle because I want to be alone."

"Yeah, I figured that."

"But you didn't figure that it counted for anything."

"Yeah, that's what I figured," Elmore said.

"Since you came all the way up here to check me out, you must have talked to Fox Vernon."

Elmore grunted.

"And since Fox didn't warn me you were coming, he must approve of this visit."

"He don't know the particulars."

"But if you tell me, I'll tell him."

"You were checking out rumors this winter that Homer White was gambling on games," Elmore said to the windshield. "I know this for a fact."

Drover held his breath. He stared out the same rain-streaked windshield and saw the streetlamps and buildings and kept waiting for Elmore to go on.

"Some guys in this business take advantage," the second man said. "We like to police it."

"That's why they gave you badges and guns," Drover said.

"We don't need badges," the second man said.

"We don't care about illegal gambling in Chicago except it can get tied in to our things. We want a casino in the Midwest. Maybe Chicago, maybe someplace else, but we got to expand," the second man said. "We don't need some shit about gambling and players messing with gambling."

"I don't follow this and I don't want to. I make you out to be someone from the Nevada Gaming Commission and I don't wanna know," Drover said.

"It's bigger than that," the second man said.

"That's my hotel up on the corner," Drover said.

"We know," the fat man said.

"And you're going to let me out," Drover said. He said it carefully, as though explaining the rules of disengagement to a ten-year-old with a gun.

"You want to look into Homer White and see what the story is there," the fat man said.

"I did that already. I didn't find a story, only rumors."

"Then you wanna look again. Talk to someone in the commissioner's office."

"The commissioner of baseball is a joke. He's not going to investigate Homer White. It wouldn't be in the best interest of the game," Drover said.

"But he would have to if you gave him names and figures."

"I don't want to know names and figures."

"You don't get it. You're the errand boy on this," the second man said.

"And you don't get it. I don't give a shit for Homer White but I'm not obsessed by him. I still think of other things while I smell the flowers. If you're not from the gaming commission then you're even less likely to be a friend of mine."

"You still think you're out of the environment?" the fat man said.

"Never was in."

"You're in gambling—"

"Sports. I cover sports for an oddsmaker. That's it."

"You investigate—"

"I cover sports for an oddsmaker. He asks my professional assessment of teams and players," Drover said.

"You're gonna go back to your room and you're gonna find a brown envelope with names and numbers in it. You're gonna get it to the guys you know on the papers and they're gonna get the heat on the owners and their commissioner—"

"Why would I do that?"

"For the good of the game," the fat man said.

Elmore stopped the car and put the shift in park. The motor chugged, the rain fell, everything in the world was changed. The football book he was writing was a million miles away.

"And what if you miscalculated? Maybe I don't carry grudges. Maybe I don't hate Homer White enough to be your gofer."

The second man just stared at him.

Rain. Motor. Night.

Elmore wouldn't turn to look at him.

The wind picked up and flung more rain against the darkened side windows.

"You remember that Homer White gave a deposition against you? When you was indicted that time? Said you was a party animal in Chicago, hanging around the joints, broads and booze, all that stuff," the second man said. It was a question but he delivered it flat like a statement.

"I don't remember that," Drover said. "I forget things." He reached for the door handle.

"Hold it," the fat man said. He was staring at Drover with those piggy eyes under the shadow of his hat.

Drover held it.

"I know about you, Drover. You had a lucky break when the D.A. dropped that indictment."

"Lucky me," Drover said.

"Homer White didn't do you no favor."

"So what? You want me to plant some dirt on him for you?"

"There's five thousand for you."

"Fuck your five thousand," Drover said.

"Not only a funny guy, a tough guy," the second man said.

Elmore shook his head.

"The brown envelope in your room. We want to read things soon. In the Chicago papers. Maybe New York. Make the commissioner look into Homer. For the good of the game."

Drover pushed the door handle. Seattle was being ruined for him. The people in the streets had suddenly spotted the little boy lying on the roof. It ended the game.

He opened the door.

"See you around, funny boy," the fat man said.

Drover slammed the door shut.

The car sped away, splashing rainwater in the gutters.

Damn.

He didn't even want to go up to his room. There'd be that brown envelope. And he'd have to open it sometime.

TWO

E IGHTEEN MONTHS earlier.

Another rainy night, this time in Caswell, Arkansas, in the middle of a southern winter.

Homer White played euchre with Junior Bidwell, Clive Darryl, and Buddy Gooch until damned near one in the morning in the Petunia Club.

The "club" was a typical Arkansas invention in which an ordinary bar disguised itself as a club by requiring "membership fees" from nonregulars dropping in. Not that it was segregated. As Homer White would put it, the nigra doctor from the hospital came in on a regular basis and didn't have to pay a membership fee each time. That's how unsegregated it was. Prejudiced was a different word altogether.

Homer and the boys were into whiskey with beer backs, belching and laughing and eating pork rinds. Homer White and his pals were razorbacks from the Arkansas hills, the same hills that had yielded the hillbillies for Al Capp's Dogpatch and Bill Clinton's presidency.

In their separate ways, they were men who had made it after

rewriting the rules in their own favor. Junior had turned his daddy's poor little old farm into an agribusiness that netted a million dollars a year. Clive was a judge now after being mayor of Caswell three times, and Buddy Gooch's real estate business involved five offices in two counties.

But when they played cards on nights like this, they liked to think they were nothing but good old country boys. They told dirty jokes, swore more in one night than they would in a month of Sundays, and lied to each other for the sheer pleasure of it.

The way Homer would remember it later, they turned to him in the last round of cards, asking after Mae and Millie in a needling sort of way that would have made him mad with anyone else.

"Quit San Francisco finally," Homer said of his ex-wife, Mae. He played the ace of clubs. "Couldn't get laid there, I guess."

The others guffawed. Homer had a sly accent that deepened in the winter around people he knew in his old hometown. But up in baseball—he always said "up in baseball," meaning north—the accent would be refined away during months on the road and in northern towns. "Heard she got on with a real estate outfit there. Doin' well. Seems ever'one from California is moving to Seattle, I don't know why."

"Maybe it's easier to get laid there."

"Could be. I guess Mae kept her looks, prolly lookin' for a man."

"You oughtn' talk about her that way."

"Aw, shit," Homer said. He grinned at them. "Mae and I never fooled each other much after we got divorced. She raised Millie and I raised cain and it's been all right by her long's I send the support check every quarter."

So it went, drinking and talking and taking apart the motives and reputations of everyone not at the table. There were always scandals in Caswell because small towns relish them. They know all the principals.

It was a good night, a good get-together, a good drinking session. It could be the drinking part went on longer than usual.

Homer White admitted later that he had been slightly overserved. The admission came after the county deputy pointed out that he had a nearly lethal .20 reading of blood alcohol when they tested him at the hospital.

And it was raining.

When Homer White was down home in the winter, every night seemed like it was raining and the best way to spend a rainy night was with cards and whiskey among friends. The same card players couldn't be rounded up every night Homer wanted company. The Juniors and Clives and Buddys had lives and wives. Homer wished sometimes that they didn't. He wanted friends, damn it, not a bunch of old buddies who had been sissified by years of marriage and going to church on Sunday. He liked himself and where he came from and liked that he could come back into Caswell as the big man and buy up three hundred hilly acres off Highway XX and live any damned way he wanted. He put on twenty pounds or so each winter, which got harder each time to take off in spring training, but that was no matter. Homer White usually felt indestructible. It was no different that November night.

Homer had a Mercedes convertible up in the barn but he favored his Ford F250 pickup truck for nights down in Caswell.

The friends parted outside the bar in the rain, making loud noises and hanging on to snatches of laughter turned on by rough kidding. They stood on the sidewalk a while in the rain, letting the warm rain wash down their faces and spot their shirts and feel just good to be standing there half drunk on a warm, dark night.

The laughter died as one after the other peeled off with good-byes and see-yous. In his shrewd way, Homer watched the others leave one by one. They had gray cars with four doors and Japanese names. Shit. They had all once been wild youths on a rampage, playing pickup ball by the rail yards. They had once had their whole lives ahead of them. And now they all drove gray Japanese cars and would have to explain themselves to the little woman back home. Shit. It was sad the way people turned out, Homer thought then.

He remembered going to his truck, taking out the ignition key, and climbing into the cab. Homer White found himself on the high bench seat of the old orange truck with a key in his hand. It took a couple of passes to get the key into the ignition lock and a couple of grindings to get the motor to catch. The truck made a truck sound, loud and boastful, and Homer flicked on all his headlamps, including the high beams and the double beams on a second light row set above the grille ahead of the radiator.

He remembered that much.

He remembered that Double X was slipperier than a hog in shit because the rain had come late, while they were still playing cards, and the blacktop was coated with oil and water, grease spots planed by rain. He had taken that road a thousand times and the familiarity of it led to his contempt for the conditions of the evening.

Besides, it was one in the morning and he had had a few. That's all he admitted to later, even when they showed him the score from his blood sample.

He knew himself he was going to drive with one eye shut because the single white line that divided the narrow, hilly blacktop had diverged into two tracks. You might follow the wrong one with both eyes open.

Half blind, he peeled down Main out of Caswell and picked up Double X on the far side of the abandoned rail yards. He had played among the trains as a boy and now the trains were gone.

Double X climbs quickly out of Caswell, cutting through scrub pines and some sturdy oak patches and twisting up along Caswell Ridge. His farm was spread out above Double X at a dirt road turn-in that led to the modern house he had built on the top of Little Hat Mountain.

He lived alone unless he brought a girl along. He was a neat man and his house was clean and masculine, with pine paneling and a pool table and a big fireplace formed from fieldstone. He did like women for a day or two or three and they liked him because he was attentive to women. But when he got tired of the girls, he just shut himself down like that and drove them to Little Rock or wherever and told them it had been fun. Just like that. He was a cold son of a bitch, everyone agreed on that, even his pals who played in the night euchre games.

He just took the turn onto his private dirt road too damned fast was all. Nobody was hurt, what was the big deal? He was practically on his own property.

What happened was the front wheels bit pea gravel and the rear skidded on the grease-and-water surface of the blacktop.

Homer White was riding the brake now and in that slow-motion second, he realized he was just going too damned fast. The pickup started to roll.

His eyes—both of them—were open as he gripped the wheel and tried to turn it away from what was happening.

What was happening was that a high-riding pickup truck with less weight over the rear axles and too much over the front was in the process of proving why race cars are not built like pickup trucks.

The truck seemed to take forever to flip.

First the right side hit the shoulder, and that was enough to give it momentum. The side of the road here slid down toward a rainwater culvert already muddy with runoff from the storm. The pickup found that depression convenient to maintain the momentum of the rollover. It continued while Homer White watched, his hands knuckle-white on the steering wheel.

The windshield shattered next as the truck's roof hit and glass flew at Homer's face while Homer flew toward the glass. The roof smacked his head and then the windshield and then it was the roof again. He never wore a seatbelt and he was flying all over the inside of the cab.

The pickup was slowing, interrupted by two ash trees that bent against the force of the rollover but wouldn't be broken. The radiator cracked, sending up a geyser of steam and the wheels kept turning like a dog's legs on ice, looking for some grip.

No grip and no luck. His legs came off the pedals and smashed hard above the knees on the underside of the steering wheel and then forced both legs into the crunch between the wheel, post, and dash.

It was over in three seconds.

Homer lay, upside down, his face cut and bleeding and his legs crushed in the vise of the wheel and dash. He couldn't see a thing because the windshield was smashed to hell and it was looking out on grass in the dark of night.

Rain. It was raining like hell.

Homer blinked his eyes.

Water ran in the culvert beneath the truck and he thought he could hear the sound of it rushing across the dead grass.

Then he thought his legs were going to be torn off.

Then he blacked out.

It rained all night long that night, eighteen months earlier.

THREE

Drover FINISHED the book on Sunday morning. The brown envelope the men in the car had talked about was in his garment bag in
the closet of the hotel room. He hadn't opened it. He was thinking
about it all the time even while he tried to decide if the scouting reports
on the San Francisco 49ers confirmed that they would be in the Super
Bowl again even if they had the groundskeepers as wide receivers. He
at last decided that and then, wonderfully, it was done.

It wasn't *War and Peace*, though Drover was pretty sure he'd get
around to writing that someday. Like all writers, he sustained himself
through the process of writing by thinking ahead to Someday.

Sunday morning was all fogged in up and down the coast. No
planes out just yet from Sea-Tac and Drover thought he did not have
an urgent need to get back just yet.

He slipped four soft disks in wraps into a Federal Express overnight
envelope and sealed it. He had four duplicate soft disks for himself.
Such was his manuscript, not even the triumphant pile of papers that

writers can point to as a sure sign that literacy has been committed recently.

He put on his raincoat and old fishing hat and went out into the fog and mailed the Federal Express package at the automatic dump box up the street. He might have called Fox Vernon to tell him he was finished but he was pissed off at Fox. Fox had no right to tell Elmore where he was. Elmore was an errand boy for an oddsmaker named Sal Marconi, who *did* have mob connections (as they say), and Drover had met him maybe a dozen times in the Vegas part of his life. Vegas is a small town for a big city and no matter what you do, you keep bumping into the same people. What bothered him at odd moments was the other guy. He knew that guy but he couldn't place him. He couldn't figure out who the other guy was and he didn't want to figure it out, but there it was, nagging at him.

He rode the monorail out to the Space Needle, walked around the shabby park a little, and then monorailed back downtown. Seattle shuts down on Sunday like most cities and the tall buildings look lonely.

The hookers began to sally out late in the afternoon, in the fog, carrying their umbrellas with them and trying not to scare the squeamish with outrageous makeup. Hookers in Seattle, unlike streetwalkers in L.A., try for a down-home look. The hotels and the hookers were looking for next week's conventioneers but the fog had grounded everything.

Drover finally settled into a sports bar down by the docks and watched the Seattle Mariners win one in the Kingdome. Baseball was a lousy television game but it was all the afternoon held. The Supersonics were playing the Bulls, but that game didn't start until 8:00 P.M. He drank a couple of Samuel Adamses with a guy who said he was from Chicago. It took about fifteen ounces of beer to determine that the guy had never set foot in the town. Drover was disappointed. He always liked to get news of the old city.

The man Not-from-Chicago moved down the bar and Drover suddenly focused again on the TV set.

It was Homer White selling basketball shoes. Weird.

Homer White was of no use to him, but he had seen the way it was for Homer, even back then, and in his way, Drover forgave him.

There was no point in building up hatreds in your life. Besides, Homer was coming to the end of his career and everyone knew the deal with Homer and how hard it was going to be for him. Homer had a reputation as a boozer and braggart who had no friends on any team, including his own. When he was no longer able to hit the ball, he'd be out of baseball faster than a Nolan Ryan strike. Pro sports, like most things, depended on a buddy network. Homer had never taken care of anyone but Homer and the payback would come when he tried to become someone's pitching coach or minor league scout.

What if whatever was in the envelope in his room was true?

Drover thought about it. He had been thinking about it all along, a buzz just below the other buzz of finishing the football book.

Fox Vernon had put Elmore and his fat friend into contact with Drover. Fox Vernon wanted to know what Elmore wanted Drover for. Was it some kind of a test? Fox was an independent oddsmaker, which meant he wasn't connected to the Outfit. Didn't he trust Drover? Did he want to see if Drover would jump for an Outfit stooge like Elmore?

Drover snapped himself out of it with a shake of his head. He wasn't going to feel sorry for Homer on top of everything else, was he? What was it to him if Homer gambled away his reputation?

But he knew. He wasn't going to do errands for Elmore Leonardo any more than he was going to give Fox Vernon the satisfaction of calling him to tell him what had transpired in the rain in Seattle. Fuck them both.

When he got back to the hotel, there was a message for him.

Some retreat Seattle was turning out to be. He might as well have locked himself in a suite in Vegas.

Drover ran his fingers through his spiky brown hair while waiting for the other end of the line to come on. He stood in the lobby at a row of pay phones because he didn't feel like going up to his room yet. The airport was backed up still, crippled by fog, and the fog was everywhere. So what was he going to do but wait it out? Read a book. Have a couple of scotches in lonely celebration of finishing the football book. Maybe more than a couple. Watch the basketball game on the tube in a friendly bar. Basketball was definitely a TV game.

The fourth ring did it.

"Hello?"

The voice was brisk but low, just the way matter-of-fact ladies sound on the line.

"This is Jimmy Drover. Someone called me."

"I called you. I'm Mae Tilson."

Mae Tilson, Mae Tilson, Mae Tilson. If it was supposed to ring a bell, Drover wasn't hearing it. He said so. It was put a little rudely because he felt ruded upon.

"I'm Homer White's wife," she said.

Drover caught his breath and held it.

"Ex-wife," she continued. Same flat tone, some low edges to it. No accent, or maybe that was the accent in Seattle. Everyone just happens to be in Seattle all of a sudden and everyone wants to talk about Homer White. Except Drover, the designated listener.

"I want to see you. I just found out you were in the city."

"How'd you find that out?"

"I got the number of your hotel room."

"Obviously. I'm returning the call. But who told you I was here?" Instead of, why are you calling me in the first place?

"Max Heubner," she said.

Max Heubner was a general partner in the extremely mediocre franchise called the Seattle Mariners. He was a Seattle real estate developer who converted sections of forest into subdivisions and arranged downtown deals. Drover knew him, had known him, and had not made contact with him in Seattle because he had happily assumed Max Heubner didn't even know he existed.

"How did Max Heubner know I was here?" Drover said.

"I don't know. He said he didn't know you but that friends or something had said you were someone to see and that you happened to be in Seattle."

"This is out of Pirandello," Drover said.

Pause.

"I don't get that," she said.

"Nothing to get, Miss Tilson. Just a smart-ass thing," Drover said.

"Well, here goes." She took an audible breath. "Max is a business friend of mine. He said you used to be a sports writer and that you were supposed to be in the private detective business now." It sounded genuine, the way she said it. Maybe he was getting paranoid. The matter-of-fact thing in the voice became a little more concerned.

"I was a writer; I'm not the other thing," Drover answered.

"You're not really a detective?"

"Not really."

"But you do things. Watch the sports world. For someone in Las Vegas. A gambler—"

"He's not a gambler, I'm not a gambler," Drover said. And he began to sound careful again. Who the hell was this voice on the phone? The FBI listening? Or IRS? Drover wondered if someone had written his name and number on a billboard.

"I try to evaluate sports for him. I'm one of his eyes on the games." Why this careful overexplanation? But he wanted to get it all on the recording if there was a recording.

"How do you evaluate Homer?"

The ex-wife had some directness at least. And she hadn't mentioned the brown envelope in the closet of his room. Maybe she had nothing to do . . . well, that was silly. We're on the phone, we're all connected, it says so in the commercials.

"I'd like to see you," she said, dropping the question of a moment earlier.

"When?"

"Right now."

"What's this about, Mae?" It was the cop's first-name familiarity. Drover had learned it from cops and how intimidating it is. He wanted to intimidate Mae because he felt someone was setting him up for a sucker punch.

That seemed to give her a longer than usual pause. When she picked it up again, her tone had changed and Drover couldn't gauge what it meant.

"About Homer. I'll be honest. He said you snooped on him last winter. That you were looking to see if he had gambling contacts."

"So?"

She drove on. "He says he knew you from years ago in Chicago. Said he saw you in the bars on Rush Street. Said he knew you because you covered the team sometimes. Look, you don't know me. It was over between Homer and me long before. I just. . . ." Another pause. "Can I buy you dinner?"

"All right," he said. Waiting and careful.

"Any favorite place?"

"Do you live in Seattle?"

"Not far."

"Then you know places better than I do."

"Then I'll pick you up at your hotel."

"When?"

"Half an hour."

Drover was intrigued and that bothered him. Everything was starting to bother him. He liked retreats, he liked being invisible from time to time, he liked to hide out in a place like Seattle and disappear off the face of the earth. Suddenly, everyone could contact him, even perfect strangers like Mae. And it was all circling back to Homer White of the Cubs. He didn't like it. He'd had a similar feeling once when he volunteered to sit on the board above a dunking tank at a carnival for charity. But no matter now. Curiosity had the upper hand.

"How will I know you? I'll be in the lobby—" Drover began.

"I'll be the woman with red hair, the pretty one," Mae said and then Drover knew right away what the tone in her voice meant.

It meant business.

FOUR

MAE WAS the pretty one.

And her hair was red.

She and he didn't say anything until they were in the Oldsmobile heading across a bridge into the foggy, foggy dark of the eastern suburbs. He had gone to his room, shaved again, and slipped on his corduroy sports jacket. His hair was uncombable as usual and he just brushed it into a sullen sort of order.

Mae was tall and she carried herself with easy grace. She was wearing slacks and a brown sweater. Her hair was cut short and it was red in a way that suggested the sunlight would give Mae freckles. If the sun was ever going to shine again in Seattle.

They both wore seat belts and Mae drove in a concentrated way, both hands on the wheel and arms straight out. The car was the top end of the Oldsmobile line, complete with leather seats. She drove the way a professional drives and she was in charge of whatever conversation they were going to have.

"Homer has troubles," Mae began.

"We all have troubles, Mae."

She glanced at him and then back to the road. "That's a little mean," she said.

"I don't owe Homer any favors. I doubt many people do." He watched her profile. She wasn't reacting. "What's your connection to him now? Or to Max Heubner?"

"Or to both of them?" she said next. See, there was no getting ahead of her in this conversation. Drover decided he would sit in his seat like a good little boy and see where she wanted to go with this.

Nowhere, it seemed. She didn't say another word for the next ten minutes. They edged into the parking lot of the little suburban restaurant with the twinkly lights around the doors and windows that say it is either Christmas or someone Italian owns the place. Good. He wanted Italian food. And he was glad to have solved the mystery of where all the people go when they leave downtown Seattle on weekends. The parking lot was jammed.

Warm wood tones, a buzz of conversation, and no Muzak. The host was a large man who took them to a small table near the back where a gas-fed fireplace did a fair imitation of one that used wood.

"Good food," she said.

"I'll be the judge of that," Drover said, taking aim at the menu.

That made her smile. Mae had killer green eyes and fashionably concave cheeks that pouted into a wide and pretty mouth. There was no one thing about her that stunned you—she didn't wear good looks like a loud dress—but there were so many little things. That smile, for instance.

Drover ran his hand once more through the dry tangle of his short brown hair and gave up on it. He would never look better than he did and that wasn't saying much. He thought the veal scallopini would be the litmus test of how good—or how Italian—the place was.

"You like Italian food?" Mae said.

"My friend Kelly has a theory about that. He says ethnic food doesn't travel west of the Mississippi. West of the Miss, Italians forget how to cook and Greeks lose their oopah. He says it's the reason everything is tofu and veggieburgers in California."

"Well, this isn't California," she said.

"But it is politically correct," Drover said.

"Trust me," Mae said. "This is authentic Italian soul food."

Mae ordered first and selected the wine without asking for concurrence. Drover noticed. She was certainly more interesting than the tell-all autobiography of the Green Bay coach he had brought along for nights alone. Maybe better than a televised basketball game.

They had the wine instead of drinks before. The waiter brought them olive oil served in a dish with a pile of Italian bread. Drover asked for *giardiniera* to spice it up and got it—another sign that they knew what they were doing in the place. He dipped the bread in oil and then put some of the green, spicy vegetables on it.

"Like it so far?" she said. He realized then that she sounded exactly like the woman who had really turned him on to Renaissance poets in his second year of college. No wonder he was beginning to like her.

She told him all about herself in a way.

"Max Heubner and I have had business dealings. I came up from San Francisco. This was the hot market and Max helped me get set up, get my license."

He put his antenna up again.

"Do you know him?" Mae said. "He knew all about you."

"Like he said. He had dealings in Chicago once when I was on the paper there. I did sports and Max was a sport." There. That didn't sound right. "Had a box at Wrigley Field. He had friends, business contacts. I never really knew him. Only what I knew in the papers. He was in development. I don't know anything about real estate." Drover waited, bread in hand. But she didn't break in.

"So now I know he's got a minority stake in the Mariners. That's all I know," Drover said.

"He's an interesting man," she said.

Now he waited. The conversational tennis game was slowing up. They both seemed to know it at the same time.

Mae said, "I'm a real estate broker and Max and I dated a few times, but we're just friends. Exactly as they say in the gossip columns," she began. She dipped the bread and tasted the extra virgin but not the giardiniera.

The wine was fine. He couldn't go beyond that. Wine was described on menus as though it were something else. Haughty or naughty or something, sometimes pretentious or portentous or something. Drover would never make it as a menu writer.

"Earthy. Like a peasant's laugh," he said, holding the glass.

"My God," she said. "Don't tell me you watch the Frugal Gourmet? He's a part of Seattle I don't admit to," she said.

That broke it a little between them. Sometimes it is just something silly like that. They talked about the Frugal Gourmet for a while and then about other things. Drover noticed they were not getting back to Max Heubner.

The food was good, just the way she said it would be. He didn't feel pressured to savor it like a gourmet at all. He felt as fine about it as he would about one of Black Kelly's legendary meat loaf dinners complete with mashed potatoes, gravy, and string beans.

He began to tell her a story or two about Black Kelly and she laughed in a low, gentle way that felt good and honest to Drover. Did she work for the feds? Was she wired? Or from the mob? He was beginning not to care.

The coffee brought up the name of Homer White again. That was a little bit sobering but it didn't destroy the good mood.

"Homer married me when I was eighteen. That sounds young but he was a boy from my hometown and eighteen isn't that young down there," she began.

She told him about Caswell, Arkansas, and about the hometown boy with blond, bluff good looks and those cobalt blue eyes who went from A-ball to the Big Show in one year. One year from Class A in Iowa to the Cincinnati Reds, where he did well enough. He was tagged to a four-player deal in the off-season with the Cubs. The Cubs sent him down to their Iowa team and it seemed that Homer had had enough of Iowa. So he took matters into his own hands. The ones that held a 35-ounce Louisville Slugger. By August, he was up in the Bigs, as the players call it. The Chicago Cubs and Wrigley Field and the adoration of the media. One year into his baseball life, he hit 39 home runs and created 109 RBIs and hell, he was just getting the hang of it, as he put it at the time.

And when the Cubs gave him all that money—nearly $15,000 a year on a two-year contract—he went back to Caswell and slept around and found out that Mae Tilson was prettier than all the others put together. They had gotten married even though her family didn't think it would last.

"They showed remarkable judgment," she said.

"It didn't last."

"It lasted long enough for a pregnancy and the birth of Millie. Millicent, named for my mother. I wanted my mother to like me. She didn't approve of Homer or his people. He was trash to her. I wanted her to like me and like the marriage and I guess I named Millie after her for all those bad reasons."

She sighed. She looked at her glass of wine and touched the stem but did not raise it. Her eyes clouded over with a covering of dreaminess. "I wanted Homer to like me. I wanted to be liked. I got over that. When I got over Homer," she said. She said it like she had said it enough times to believe it.

"Everyone wants to be liked."

"I want to make it clear, Drover." She used his last name instead of his first as though he were a recruit and she were the general. He noticed she had long fingers and red nails. He kept noticing little things about her. Like her neck. Nice neck. He just knew he'd never make it as a menu writer.

"Like a beautiful swan's neck," he said.

She stopped as though she understood. She waited out the requisite silence.

"I want to make it clear that I have no romantic attachment to either Max or Homer. This is about business and I'm the middleman. You might say I've been middled by circumstances."

"Why?"

"Because general partners of baseball teams can't talk to men like you. Detectives. Look at the trouble George Steinbrenner got into," she said.

He made a face then. He put his napkin on the table as though dismissing something. "Steinbrenner got the shaft when baseball had a commissioner. Baseball is not into commissioners anymore, no matter what he's called. Baseball is getting into the game it does best, which is owner's greed matched by player's greed. Max doesn't want to talk to me? Fine. I'd much rather talk to you. But don't take too much of what Max says as gospel or even vaguely true. Max is full of shit, like all self-made men."

That got color in her cheeks. "Max is a friend of mine."

"Fine. But don't make me out to be something I'm not. I'm not a gambler or a detective or a member of the crime syndicate. I am just a guy getting through and if someone wants something from me, he personally has to ask for it. Although, as I said, I'd much rather talk to you," Drover said.

"Then you don't want to hear what I have to say?"

"I do." No, that wasn't true. But he was going to listen to her because he had wine and the room was romantic and she had killer eyes.

"Homer has troubles. I told you that. He's in the middle of a six-year contract. He signed it before the accident."

"He flipped his pickup truck or something in Arkansas," Drover recalled. "Broke a couple of bones. When was it? Winter before last."

"In his legs. Broke his legs. But he's strong. He's the strongest person I've ever known. He healed up in three months."

"That's wonderful," Drover said.

"You don't have to be sarcastic."

"I'm not a fan. Homer White is edging toward the twilight of his career. He is now making $1.5 million annually from the Chicago Cubs, for which he hit .221 or thereabouts last year and hit 13 home runs. Homer has lost his homer. That's what I would write if I did those things anymore. He's got a big long contract that the Cubs might like to dump on someone but who would want it?"

"Max Heubner would," Mae said.

That was intriguing enough for Drover to keep his mouth shut.

"Max wants Homer White. A designated hitter. The Mariners don't have a hitter."

"They don't have a lot of things."

"Look, is this confidential? I mean, your code of ethics? As an investigator?"

Why was she convinced he was a detective when he told her he wasn't? Maybe people see the truths they want to see. He nodded a lie at her. "Sure, this won't go beyond you and me if you want."

"All right." Her eyes appraised him a moment longer and then she sipped her coffee.

"Homer's legs. He has tremendous pain. The longer the season, the more the pain. He can't stand for 162 games a year anymore, it's as simple as that."

"From the accident."

"It has to be. Joint pain. Arthritis."

"The Cubs know this?"

"Sure."

"And the Mariners know this?"

She nodded.

"And the general partner of the Mariners wants a crippled-up thirty-nine-year-old hillbilly with bad wheels to hit thirteen homers a year for them?"

"To hit .313 for them," she said. "Max and the general manager think that Homer will hit his weight in gold for the Mariners if he can become a DH."

"The American League. Everyone's old-age retirement home."

"He can still hit, it's the pain all the time. And they are running him ragged in Chicago and—"

"Now, Mae—if I can call you Mae when you keep calling me Drover—Mae, I want to ask you one question."

She waited for it.

He took his time, traced a line on the tablecloth, tried to look like a professional. He even frowned before he relaxed into a grin. It wasn't a nice sort of grin, not the kind that anticipates humor. More like a lie.

"What's this really about?"

"You think I've just been lying to you?"

"Something like that."

"Then you and I don't have anything to talk about."

"Not if you don't want to stop lying."

The color in her cheeks was anger this time. Her green killer eyes got greener, the way a cat's eyes change when it stops playing with the mouse and settles down to business.

Drover watched the change in her. It was as though she had decided some terrible thing and now was waiting to carry it out.

39

"Look," he began again. He looked at his wine glass so that he did not have to look at her eyes. "How is it that I would figure in anything to do with whether Homer White comes to Seattle and the American League or stays with the Cubs?"

But it was really too late. He looked up and her eyes told him that.

"Check," she said suddenly and there was someone at her elbow handing over the bill. And she covered it without looking with a gold American Express card. When the waiter went away, she said it in a low, cold voice:

"I know what you are, Drover. I was trying to be polite. You got fired from a paper because you talked to the wrong people once. I know what you are is a stupid, bitter man who does odd jobs for a Vegas bookmaker and pretends to watch sports for a living. What you are is a lowlife who lives like a bum on a pier in California and does as little as possible for a living. And for other people."

"But I'm ornamental," Drover said.

"I don't see it. Max Heubner sent me because he said you were a good man, decent, that you got a bad break once and that you were sort of like an unofficial policeman to sports now. Keeping things honest. What they're doing to Homer isn't honest. They know it and he knows it. He's willing to step out of the contract and try it on his own, go to Seattle to give it a shot."

"Sure. Walk away from a guaranteed million and a half a year for the next—what is it—four years, and go try out for the Mariners with no guarantees—"

"Andre Dawson did it from Montreal to the Cubs—"

"So you know baseball. Well, I knew Andre Dawson and Homer is no Andre Dawson. But you don't know Homer very well, do you?"

"Homer is a changed man since the accident."

"Changed?"

She stared right through him. She might have been talking to herself now. "He told me he quit drinking, quit messing around. You know, I didn't believe him. Then I told Max and Max checked him out and it was true. Homer is getting his act together. Just happens it comes a little late. I mean, for him and me." Her pretty mouth formed a bitter line. Drover had seen that line on the mouths of a lot of women with regrets.

"And that's why your friend Max wants to bring him to Seattle?"

"You don't understand. It has to do with the Cubs' management. The general manager is Eddie Briggs and the Mariners have talked to him about a trade for Homer. Except Eddie puts the price too high. And then, when Homer went to talk to him about it, he denied that he had even talked to Seattle—"

"It's called lying, Mae. It's done all the time."

"But why would the Cubs keep Homer when he's not doing it for them but he could get a new life in the American League? The DH rule was made for someone like Homer."

"But why you, Mae? And why me?"

"Eddie Briggs is the key. And you know Chicago. You could find out about what it is that Eddie has on Homer that he wants to keep him twisting in the wind this way."

"I don't know anything about Eddie Briggs and Homer White. Eddie was a manager in Milwaukee and before that a mediocre second baseman. Hell, maybe Homer beat him up once in a bar and Eddie is holding a grudge." Drover smiled to show that he was kidding.

But Mae wasn't smiling. "It's something like that. You have to find out."

"I don't."

"Homer—what's being done to him isn't right. He's a changed man, Drover. Really changed."

"Oh, God, another deathbed conversion. Does he make the sign of the cross now when he bats or does he still think that's just a thing spics do to make you mad?"

She slapped him then, not a silly slap at all but one that hurts without doing permanent damage. His left nostril began to bleed and he picked up his napkin to stop it.

She was on her feet.

"You're a shit," Mae said.

Turned and walked toward the door.

He thought to call her back. Tell her it was a mistake and he wasn't a shit.

After all, as he'd told her, everyone wants people to like them. All except Mae Tilson, because she said so.

But he just sat there, holding a napkin to his nose. He thought he was going to have to separate out whatever was true and whatever was false in Mae Tilson's story. That slap had been true. It was hard and it hurt. And that was just for starters. Those two suits in the green Caddy the other night were just preamble to Mae's story.

FIVE

MONDAY DROVER flew home.

Home is where they have to take you in, and he really didn't
know if his home met that definition. He had drifted into Santa Cruz
one dazed day seven years ago, looking for a drink and a couple of
days of sun on the public beach. Instead, he found the improbable
Black Kelly. They talked about Chicago childhoods, played chess, and
talked politics. Kelly, the firehouse cook, had sealed their friendship
with a display of barbecued baby back ribs and sweet potatoes in onions
that was just short of sinful. He had a vacant apartment in the back
of the saloon and Drover paid two months rent. He expected to move
on but he never did.

They were both drifting through time and they knew it and living
on the pier at Santa Cruz was just a form of drifting on. They became
friends without meaning to do it.

Kelly picked him up at SFX at noon in the big black Cadillac he
called the bus. He came from a family of redheads but he had black
oily hair and eyes as blue as Galway Bay. "Black" Kelly—to distinguish

him from his red-haired siblings—stuck after a while and no one called him by his Christian name anymore.

"All done," Kelly grunted in greeting.

"I got into a situation at the end," Drover said, slumping into the passenger seat.

"Involving a woman."

"Yes, but not that way."

"Is it a bad thing?"

"Yes. At least I think so."

"Do you need my professional advice?"

"Yes."

The car swung south. The day was clear and cool and great stands of California pines filled the hillsides all the way down to the sea. Archeologists are wrong: The Garden of Eden was originally in northern California before Adam and Eve began screwing it up.

Drover told him the fragments of incidents and Kelly listened in his judicious way, staring out the windshield as if gazing at his estate. He drove with one hand on the wheel and a seatbelt that straightened across his grizzly-bear chest and belly.

When Drover was done, Kelly let the silence ride a while. Then he said: "Someone wants to get Homer White."

"Remarkable, Watson."

"The question is, who and why? Also how?"

"Not why. Homer White's got so many reasons to be gotten it's a wonder he's not dead yet. He's a stupid hillbilly racist womanizing son of a bitch, for starters."

"Other than that, how did you like the play, Mrs. Lincoln?"

"I don't like him."

"I gather that."

"So why would people in Seattle suddenly be coming to me to do something about him? His ex-wife somehow wants me to save him by getting him traded to Seattle, where he can enjoy life as a designated hitter. What am I, his priest? Why would I do him a favor if I could? And what exactly was I supposed to do?"

"You apparently didn't give the lady a chance to tell you."

"That is some lady, Kelly."

"You didn't really describe her except to say she was pretty. But then, you say that to all the women."

"They are all pretty."

"Well, you made the lady walk before you could find out what was on her mind," Kelly said.

"What was on her mind was some theory about the Cubs' general manager holding a grudge against Homer. Nice grudge. He's making a million and a half a year on a contract that was a giveaway even before Homer flipped his truck. The thing about Mae Tilson was I kept believing her and then not believing her. It changed moment to moment."

Kelly said. "What was in the brown envelope?"

"I haven't opened it."

They were up in the hills now and the ocean was down there on the right, crashing onto the white beaches littered with tanned bodies. Up here the air is thinner and colder and more bracing, scented with pines.

"You think all of them are connected? The gofer Elmore and the fat guy? And the lady and the general partner?" Drover asked his friend.

"We'll have to wait for Oliver Stone to make another conspiracy picture," Kelly said.

"What should I do?"

"Remember when you put things off? You're kidding yourself, kid," Kelly said. "You know what you should do."

"And why did Fox Vernon set me up in Seattle? You and he were the only two guys who knew where I was. I trusted Fox and he let me down. Twice."

"Maybe only once. I mean, if the four people in Seattle are all connected."

"Max Heubner consorting with known gamblers? I think even that ninety-seven-pound weakling of a commissioner would have to think hard about that one," Drover said.

"The way to find out why Fox Vernon did what he did is to ask him. And the first thing to do is to open the brown envelope and see what's inside. And the second thing is to figure out who to give it to."

"I don't want to know about Homer White. I want to be left alone—"

"C'mon. You're always stickin' your neck out for people. Like Nancy that time. And Fionna in Chicago that time. And—"

"Homer White is a shit and I probably owe him a good deal less than nothing and if I could stick a knife in him without a comeback, well . . . I'd think about doing it." Then, in a more quiet voice: "But I don't want to go back to all that."

"All what?" Kelly turned away from the road and looked at his friend. It was Drover's turn to stare straight ahead.

"When the federal attorney in L.A. went after me to prove I was corrupting my paper by consorting with known criminals and getting in on fixing games, Homer White was called to offer a deposition on what he knew about me."

"He knew you?"

"When I was starting out with the Chicago paper, before I jumped to the L.A. paper, I knew those guys. Homer White wasn't my best friend but I'd see him partying. I partied down on Divison Street and so did he. We had a few drinks here and there. In those days, I carried a toothbrush with me when I went down to Divison Street on Friday nights. You know?"

"The good old pre-AIDs days."

"Homer gave his deposition. It wasn't much and it was mostly true. About how much I spent, how much I drank, guys I would bump into. There were some bad guys I grew up with in the old neighborhood, you know that."

"You can't help who you grow up with."

"The federal attorney was doing a number on me for publicity. I was named in the indictment along with two dozen men with Sicilian names to show he wasn't prejudiced, that he got an Anglo. And a newspaperman on top of it. The paper canned me and then the indictment against me was dropped because it wasn't worth the paper it was written on. But a newspaper can never admit a mistake and they didn't take me back. So I sued them. And I won. But that ended my newspaper career."

He had recited it just like that before. Kelly had heard it, of course. But he never interrupted. It would be like breaking in on another's mantra. Or prayer. Each sentence was flat, immutable, terrible. He was a man reciting how his own life came to an end. All he had ever wanted was to be a newspaperman, just like all Kelly ever wanted to be was a Chicago fireman. They had both been stripped of the objects of their desire. Drover was cut off from it by a stupid federal prosecutor in L.A. and Kelly's career ended when half a wall in a burning building fell down and broke his back.

"So you're not inclined to do Homer White any favors because of something that happened ten years ago," Kelly said.

"Something like that. He was ordered to give a deposition and it put him in a spot. He was hitting like a blue streak for the Cubbies then but they weren't paying for it. The big-salary days were just coming in and he was hanging on and hungry and the last thing a team as stuffy as the Cubs want to hear about is that one of their players might be hanging around with gamblers and whores. So he gave the deposition and they kept it quiet and when the indictment was dropped, he tried to call me to apologize because he had had to do it. I told him I didn't care what he had to do, I just didn't want to talk to him anymore. I was getting ready to sue the paper then and I was just sick of it, all the time. I went around throwing up into brown paper bags all day."

"On the other hand," Kelly said with a gentle growl, "you don't want to hurt him either."

"I don't want to hurt myself. Why is a two-bit gofer for an Outfit oddsmaker driving a Mr. X down a rainy street in Seattle looking for me? This does not bode well for Jimmy Drover," Drover said.

"Always thinking of yourself."

Nancy Harrington was Kelly's friend. It wasn't supposed to turn out that way when it started. Drover was the one in love with the Vegas songbird who got into bad trouble with a weasel professional poker player. When Nancy was threatened, Drover was the knight who rode the white horse to rescue her. But Kelly was the best friend who got the girl.

He and Nancy were as discreet as they were in love. Neither talked about marriage or about living together even. It was just a slow something that glowed between them.

Nancy was sitting at the big round back table and Toby was behind the bar, but otherwise Kelly's saloon was empty at three in the Monday

47

afternoon when the owner and his pal arrived. The sun was bright but the air was nippy in Santa Cruz, and the beaches were deserted between the pier itself and the boardwalk amusement park.

Nancy gave Drover her sisterly kiss but didn't kiss Kelly. Kissing was something they did in private.

Sal in the kitchen scrambled eggs and summer sausage and made hash browns with onions mixed in them. There was enough cholesterol in the meal to give a plowhorse a heart attack and the two men thoroughly enjoyed it.

Halfway through a postmeal Scotch on the rocks, Drover took the brown envelope out of his bag and dropped it on the table. He looked at Kelly and Nancy and then said, "What the hell."

"It could be another draft notice," Kelly said, slitting open the envelope with his finger. "I remember my draft notice disappointed me because it didn't say 'Greetings.' It said 'Greeting.' I still get bothered by that." He shook out the papers.

"Xerox," Drover said, turning over the pages.

"Of what?"

"Betting slips. Alleged betting slips. Nice and neat and small handwriting, just like a bookie's."

"With Homer's name on them."

"Obviously."

"Are they real?"

"Only his hairdresser knows for sure."

"Then what are they worth?"

"Everything and nothing. They aren't evidence. But they could warrant asking a few questions."

"So send them to the commissioner's office and wash your hands of it."

"Why me? If they had these things, why didn't *they* send them to the commissioner's office? They want me to pass them along to my ex-buddies on various newspapers. And they want to give me five grand for my trouble."

"And you don't want to."

"Look at this."

It was a photograph. One of the men was obviously Homer White in civilian clothes. He was sitting in a leather-lined booth in some kind of restaurant or lounge. There were drinks on the table. There were two other men. One smoked a big cigar. One faced the camera. The one smoking the cigar was an Outfit guy from Chicago named Tony Ricci. The other guy was the man in the hat in the green Cadillac in Seattle, the fat man.

"Shit," Drover said. "I get it now. This is a setup."

"What's a setup?"

"This was one of the guys in the car in Seattle. That goombah there is Tony Ricci."

"And the other guy is Homer White, right?"

"Which means this is a good pasteup job or it's real. In any case, they've dumped it on me and given me this little bit of drama to impress on me that they are very dangerous people to cross. So they want me to errand-boy this stuff to guys in the press who wouldn't take the time of day from the likes of them but might take it from me."

"To get Homer White."

"I told you. Lots of guys would like to get Homer White for lots of reasons."

"What are you going to do?"

Drover sat there and thought about it. Then he picked up his scotch and tasted it and thought about it some more.

"I think I'm going to dump this in the ocean," Drover said.

Kelly waited, his big hands resting in a prayerlike attitude on the table, thick fingers laced in thick fingers.

"On the other hand, maybe they would dump me in the ocean."

"Call Fox Vernon," Nancy said.

They both looked at her. Of course. It was so obvious and they had both been thinking way beyond the obvious.

Kelly brought the phone to the table. A hustler's bar always has a phone with a thirty-foot cord on it for regulars. Drover dialed the number in Vegas and got the woman who answered to patch him through. The next voice belonged to Fox Vernon.

"How's Seattle, Drover?"

"I'm back in Cruz, Fox."

"Good. The book is done?"

"Done and in the mail."

Silence.

49

"What's on your mind?" Fox said then. He was the kind of nervy, restless type who really didn't indulge in small talk. Because he was involved in sports gambling, he lived and worked in Las Vegas because sports gambling is legal there. But he was the most un-Vegas person you would ever meet, from his Brooks Brothers button-down shirts to his pallid, emotionless round face.

"Nothing. I thought I'd tell you the book was finished."

"Good. You need a check right away?"

"It doesn't matter," Drover said.

They waited some more. Fox never waited in a phone conversation, but he was waiting this time and Drover was letting him.

"Well, when will I see you again?" Fox said.

Drover said nothing.

"Hello, you there?"

"I'm here.

They waited some more.

"Did Elmore Leonardo find you?"

"He found me."

"What's it about?"

"You don't know?"

"I don't know."

"So why'd you send a guy like Elmore Leonardo to find me?"

"Because I had to."

"Why's that?"

"Because he said he had something on a ballplayer who was going to be kicked out of baseball and I wanted to know who it was and he said he would tell you and I could find out if you wanted to tell me. Elmore Leonardo was not talking about violence. This was about information and I want information. Baseball season is two weeks old and something like this could crash a team. I don't want to set lines on baseball teams when they know something I don't know."

"That's reasonable, Fox, you cold-blooded bastard," Drover said in a friendlier voice.

"So who is it?"

"I'm not going to tell you."

"You work for me."

"I do jobs for you. It's not the same thing. If you don't like the arrangement, tell me."

"I don't like not knowing what you know. Especially if it comes from a character in the environment." Fox paused.

"Who else wanted to get hold of me?"

"What?"

"Who else did you tell I was in Seattle?"

Pause.

"No one." There was a surprise in his voice.

"Is that the truth or what?"

"I never lie. You know that. I tell the truth even to myself."

"Then I'll think about it, Foxy."

"Think about what?"

"When and if I tell you anything. Or if and when I'm going to keep working on jobs for you." He hung up before Fox Vernon could speak to that.

"Did you get an answer?" Kelly said.

Drover looked at him and then at Nancy. He began to slip the papers back into the envelope.

"What are you going to do?"

Drover put the envelope back into his garment bag. He reached for the paper and began to turn to the sports section.

"See where the Cubs are playing," he said. And that wasn't the answer Kelly expected at all.

SIX

HOMER WHITE and Helen Brown were the oddest couple in the world.

First of all, they had seen each other for sixteen months. Second, she had turned down his marriage proposal a half dozen times. Third, she brought him to church on Sunday, though he never sang songs or said the prayers. Fourth, he had quit drinking. Fifth, she wouldn't even live with him but they did manage to have sex. Only now Homer called it making love.

Helen Brown had smiling eyes and a quiet voice and long black hair. She liked Homer and was halfway to reforming him without meaning to.

Homer was all the way in love.

Helen Brown worked at the Rehabilitation Institute of Chicago and she had brought Homer back from his crippling injuries. She had forced him to walk when he wanted a shot to kill the pain in his legs.

She made him stretch when he wanted to crawl into a hole and just die. She made him stand up when he wanted to lie down.

She had shown him, for the first time in his life, that he might have courage. He had really never thought about such a thing.

Which led to other things. It led to his falling in love with this therapist in a white nurse's uniform with her crisp, starched good looks and gentle voice and firm hands. Walk, walk, walk, she'd say and he tried his damnedest.

And on some days, he just broke down and cried. And then he knew he would have to try that much harder because she had seen him cry. Once, she wiped tears from his eyes and he knew he would simply love her as he had never loved anyone in his life.

Love was complicated for both of them.

"I don't think I never been in love," Homer said one night when they shared her apartment and a homemade meal.

"Maybe you aren't now," Helen said in her gentle way.

"No, honey, they say you know it when you in it and thass the truth," Homer said.

He looked at her for a long time. "I like everythin' in the world all of a sudden. I like the sun and stars and moon and all that stuff. I like this meal, Helen, it was the best meal I ever had. I like it now when you smile and shake your head, just the way you shake your head. You see, Helen? This is hopeless for me and we gotta do somethin' about it."

"There's no hurry," she said then.

"Helen, I don' wanna waste a day of the rest of our life."

The things he said were compliments, all of the things he said. They came from his heart. She was sure of that. She had seen him in rehab, day after painful day, bringing his atrophied muscles back. She saw the sweat and the fear in his eyes and the times when a black beast tore his spirit down. She had heard him cry and she had held his hand while he cried it all out. She knew him well enough to know the things that he said to her came from a heart he never knew he had.

But what if she wasn't equal to the response he expected.

Or the response he needed?

"Homeboy," she called him sometimes. It was a teasing nickname and it made him blush with pleasure because it was a nickname, after all, and suggested intimacy. "I want to be careful. For your sake and mine. I was married once too. Way too young. It was a bad thing. For him and for me. And we've got problems, you and me."

"We got no problem," he would insist, shaking his head. "Ain't no problem you can't overcome. You showed me that. Still show me that."

But it was hard to do, this thing he wanted so badly. It was complicated by who he was and what he had been. And who she was.

The Cubs were playing the Colorado Rockies in Mile High Stadium. The place is built for football, so when they slipped in a baseball game, what should be a sideline becomes left field. A very short left field. Oddly, it was not the kind of night that should have suited Homer White.

The air was mountain cool and the front range of the Rockies was on parade behind the city. The stadium is right downtown and it was full of Denverites who didn't want to go home early tonight.

Homer White stroked his first home run of the evening right over the short left-field wall and winced as he trotted around the bases. Because the phenomenon of major league ball was new to Denver, Homer White's blow against the Rockies evoked a few cheers on its own. And the fans didn't throw the ball back on the field as they do in Chicago when the opposing team has a homer. In that, they showed their sophistication.

When he came up in the fourth, he was hurting bad. Shooting pains in his legs, above and below the knees, radiated into a generally uncomfortable warmth in his groin.

Helen Brown was still recommending exercises and he was still doing them. But at least two doctors said his trauma had induced arthritis that, in turn, was putting different pressure on different joints uninjured in the truck rollover. In other words, there was pain and there were pills but sometimes pills can't be used. Homer had a great eye and good reflexes with a bat, and the pills would interfere with that.

He might just have to learn to live with the pain.

He had taken too many pills the season before. Then he had talked to the new general manager, Eddie Briggs, about sending him to the American League. Briggs had said, "I'd like nothing better than to get rid of you and your contract but no one wants you."

That's when he knew Briggs would hang on to him for the rest of his career. Because Briggs was flat out lying to him. Mae had told him that when they talked on the phone. Briggs was a no-good son of a bitch and Homer might have reflected that in the old days, it took one to know one. But if Helen induced a gentle reflectiveness in their intimacy, it didn't extend to the rest of the world. Not yet. Eddie Briggs was a miserable son of a bitch.

SEVEN

D ROVER MET Rusty in the press box before the Denver game and tried to get a read on Homer White. The brown envelope of incriminating Xerox copies and the photograph were back in Santa Cruz. He hadn't thrown them into the ocean after all. He had given the picture to a pal in the photography department at the university in Santa Cruz to see if he could determine if it was fake.

William Rust had helped him break in on the Chicago paper a million years ago. He had shown him the ways of the press box and the locker room. He had shown Drover patience, how to go for the long season instead of the short hit. Rusty was still a friend and mentor and probably the best baseball reporter in the country.

Rusty chewed cigars these days instead of smoking them but nothing else had changed about the big man. He still ate like a horse, drank like a fish, and committed other animal acts appropriate to a loud man living life in a loud voice.

And behind the bluff loudness was the essential Rusty: a reporter with the eyes and hands of a brain surgeon.

"Homer belongs in the American League. I know it and the general manager knows it, but Homer is his own worst enemy. He's spent his life being a mean prick, for one thing. The black players resent him because he is a pretty open racist. And the Cubs need someone in left field now that José Marcedos decided to go back to Puerto Rico and be a pig farmer."

"Why doesn't he quit if he's hurting so bad?"

"I dunno. I talked to him in spring training and he said the pain wasn't bad, he'd taken care of himself during the winter. He looked good, in fact. But I can see him, especially on damp days like this. He's hurting. They got pills for him but that throws off his hitting. He's still got it, kid. Got the eye, got the feel of it. He can hit like he was nineteen years old again."

"What if I told you that someone wanted him? I mean, in the A.L.?"

Rusty rolled the unlit cigar in his mouth and leaned back. His blue eyes twikled as he beheld his one-time protégé. The two men were smiling at each other.

"I might buy you a steak dinner if you're in town tomorrow."

"I think I will be."

"We could eat at the Denver Press Club," Rusty said.

"Seattle."

"I never heard no such thing," Rusty said, sitting up straight. He leaned close to Drover in confidence. "Is this very good or semi-good?"

"Semi-good. Someone who knows one of the general partners says the general partner wants Homer for DH but Chicago doesn't want to let him go."

"The Cubs would need someone for left field. They could shift over Sanchez and put in a right fielder, but Seattle doesn't have shit to offer them."

"Seattle could offer to take over a six-million-dollar contract. If Homer sees it through to the bitter end, the Cubs are out six mill."

"Chickenfeed. We live in the era of the thirty-million-dollar man. Homer's contract was long on security but short on smarts. He could have gotten more. Except, as it turns out, he had a truck accident and that makes the contract look better for him."

"Six mill is never chickenfeed, even to Frank Perdue."

"Tell me the name of this Santa Claus."

Drover stared at Rusty for a moment. "Heubner."

"Heubner? Max Heubner? Why would he want to do Homer White a favor? Or the Cubs?"

"Maybe he thinks it would be to his advantage."

"And who does he sell this crazy idea to? There is more than one partner—"

"You know how it goes. Homer White might be a stupid son of a bitch but he could be a draw as a DH. Especially if he started hitting again."

Rusty stared at him for a long time and then shook his head as slowly as an old lion shaking the life out of some dead gazelle. Shaking and shaking, sure and sad.

"No, kid. It don't wash," Rusty said. "I been around forty years. I can smell it when they're fading. We all fade. I don't light my cigars anymore because I want to hang on a while longer. But Homer's got the smell to him. He's dead meat or dying and he wants to hang on but it doesn't matter. The wheels go on you, I don't care what sport, and you're dead. Games are about wheels, not arms or eyes or anything else. He can hit but there might not be a market for another DH. Who does it now for Seattle?"

"I ran it down. They've got Chiti, the old ex–first baseman. He's hitting .245 for them and he whiffs one out of five. Some DH."

"But Homer is . . . well . . . he's damaged. He plays in pain."

"Then why would Heubner want him? Even if Heubner is a dumb shit, which he isn't?"

"Because a lot of things. But start with the simplest thing, kid."

"What's that, Rust?"

"Maybe you're just wrong."

Drover stared at him.

"Maybe you're just wrong in the first place that Heubner or anyone wants Homer White anymore."

EIGHT

THE REPORTERS sat in the press box and watched the game, sometimes with naked eyes in real time through the window wall to the field below and sometimes on TV screens. The pencil guys used laptop computers to compose words on what they saw and the columnists sucked their thumbs as they thought of new ways to describe the contest of gladiators. One hundred sixty-two regular-season games a year, not counting spring training and not counting postseason, takes it out of everyone connected with baseball. The games are long, the season is long, everything is too damned long. The theater of the game was lost over the years in exaggerations. Pitchers pitch slow, posing on the mounds of the leagues, staring down the sixty-foot alley to the plate, contemplating their posterities. Batters bat the same way, taking times out between pitches to adjust their crotches, wipe their hands with resin and dirt, say their Hail Marys. And the reporters watch it all and try to give it meaning. How many ways can you say a player missed a called third strike or that a double play was made into a thing of beauty?

The play-by-play yackers commented on the action of this particular game between the Chicago National League club and the one from the city of Denver. They delivered up stats and gossip and trivia as though every moment were precious. Tonight's crowd of 41,389 ate peanuts and Cracker Jacks but did care whether they would ever come back along about the fifth inning. That's when the game was over and everyone knew it. But, like kabuki theater, it had to go on the required length of time until the fat lady made her appearance.

By the fifth inning, Homer White had cracked two of the hits he was named after and driven in four of the Cubs' eight runs. The Rockies were staggering out there and it was time to go to bed for a large segment of the population. They began streaming for the exits. Major league ball was new to Denver but the locals had caught on fast. When a team is down by eight runs in the middle of the game, it is a good time to call it a night.

Homer White thought so too.

He benched himself in the fifth and would not stay to see the rest of the game. He went down the tunnel into the locker room under the stadium stands. The equipment manager was watching the game on TV. He said hi and kept watching. Homer went to his stall and slowly, somewhat painfully, took off his clothes.

His legs were scarred where surgeons had cut him open. There was another cut on his back and another on his chest where the windshield glass had scarred him. A white-line scar just missed his left eye. His blue cold eyes were squinting now because of all the pain. It seemed to hurt more because he was naked.

He went into the other room, where they kept the showers and the whirlpool equipment. He slipped into the whirlpool and it took a while. He just closed his eyes and felt the water and tried to think of Helen Brown back in Chicago. Helen Brown was his mantra on the road. He could think of her, conjure her in his mind's eye, and she would comfort him.

When he opened his eyes, the locker room was still quiet, the game was still on, and Drover was sitting there on a stool next to the whirlpool.

They hadn't seen each other for ten years at least. They stared at each other and listened to the water gurgling in the whirlpool.

"Two guys met me in Seattle. One is connected, maybe both of them are," Drover began. No preamble.

"What the fuck are you talking about?" The growl was as surly as he could make it.

"Two guys met me in Seattle. One or both are connected with people in the crime syndicate. The Mafia. The Outfit. Wise guys. Capeesh? They gave me an envelope full of stuff that looks like gambling slips with your name on them. Also an eight-by-ten picture of you sitting in a booth in a lounge with a mobster from Chicago named Ricci. Also another guy."

They waited and listened to the water gurgle. Homer looked down at the dark water.

"My legs are killing me," he said.

"I heard."

"I can take pills and they help but they throw me off. That was last year. I don't want to do it again this year."

"You don't want to screw the Cubs out of their money when you're falling down on the job," Drover said. "You are becoming a considerate man in your old age. You probably don't even ride with the KKK anymore."

"I don't do anything with nigras, never did, just wanna be left alone. Hell, in Caswell, this place I drink at, they let in nigras all the time," Homer said. "Was this nigra doctor operated first on my leg. Not that I blame him for my pain, he did his job."

"That's white of you, Homer."

"I ain't fuckin' around, Drover. Whatever these guys gave you is bullshit. Why was it in Seattle?"

"Why indeed." Not even a question. Drover sat there with flat, sullen eyes and looked at the great white body and the crinkled brownish face and the white scar-line on his cheek.

"You gonna finally set me up because of that deposition ten years ago, was it? I tol' you, there was nothing I could do about that. Besides, you got off, didn't you?"

"No thanks to you."

"They had me by the balls. You know what kind of an outfit the Cubs are. They'da traded me if the gummint had said I was hurting their investigation."

"So it was you or me and I lost. I don't carry a grudge that long, Homer. I did hear last winter that you were involved in gambling and I looked into it. I have good sources."

"All them Mafia guys you grew up with."

"I grew up with cops too. And a couple of lawyers. Anyway, I dropped it. There wasn't anything there. It had come up because there were rumors you were dogging it last year, coming off your injury."

"Fuck! Dogging it? I never dogged shit in my life, you asshole." Now he heaved himself up from the tub and the pain of the movement crossed his face and Drover could see it. Then he saw the scars on the knees and shins. Surgical scars and other kinds of scars.

"Cut you up bad," Drover said. His voice was still flat but it wasn't hard this time.

"Cut me up bad," Homer White said. Swung out of the tub balanced on the heels of his hands. Took a step. Winced. Took another step. Reached for a towel and wrapped it around his body. His body had always been thick to support the muscles at his shoulders but now it was thicker. He was getting near the big four oh and it was showing on him.

"You don't know any mobsters in Chicago?"

"I meet guys all the time," Homer said. "When was this picture supposed to be taken?"

"I dunno."

"Then I dunno either. You meet a clown and he wants to have someone take a picture with you and you do it."

"I thought baseball players were beyond that kind of thing. I thought they sold their autographs now."

"They do, Drover, they do."

He was toweling his body with a second white towel and his muscles still rippled and you couldn't deny that he was hurting more than a man should be hurting.

"You know what baseball is. It's a shit game but it's the only game in town. Ain't no team no more. Ain't no loyalty. Shit, I been on the Cubs most of my career—they ought to mount me and put me in a freak show for that."

Drover watched him.

Homer White padded on damp feet into the locker room. Drover got up from his stool and followed him. The equipment manager was gone from the room.

"If it isn't fun, why keep doing it?" Drover said.

Homer turned to look at him. His scowl fit the ice-blue eyes perfectly.

"Baseball is about money and I was slow gettin' my share but I'm gettin' it now and I ain't givin' it back to nobody."

"I heard you'd be willing to cancel your contract right now to try out for another team. In the other league. Be a DH for any money."

"You heard that?"

There was a sly change in the man. Something about voice and eye and the fact that he had stopped toweling. Or maybe he was just dry.

"I heard that. I said I didn't believe it. Homer White would sooner marry a black woman than give up one nickel."

"What you heard about Homer White mostly, old horse, is a lot of shit being put out by a lot of gutless puppies who hit their weight and think they're worth six million a year. Ruin this game. Look at that Denver pitcher tonight. Fat slob. Man's twenty-seven years old and makes three, four million a year and he couldn't do a situp to save his sorry-ass life. Probably didn't feel like pitchin' tonight. Bunch of pouty-ass pups we got now—this game is gone to hell."

"You must of made enough, Homer. Walk away from it. You don't need all this pain."

"I need what I need and I don't need any man to tell me what it is. Mah terms, boy. Homer White terms. Homer White rules."

"Partying down on Division Street still? Or you slowed down?"

"I don't party no more."

"Why's that?"

"Because I met someone don't want me to ruin myself."

Drover had not expected that. Not at all. He stood up and crossed the concrete floor and stood about an arm's length away from Homer.

"I won't do to you what you did to me. That's sort of the golden rule inside out," Drover said. "But if you are doing some shit, gambling and fucking around, then I'm going to tell you that someone wants your ass."

"People been badmouthin' me since I was a young'un. I don't pay them no mind. They're worthless trash, all of them."

"You ever think all those people bad-mouthing you might be on to something?"

Homer turned then and walked into his stall. There were no lockers, only stalls divided by panels, with street clothes hung on hangers. His dirt- and sweat-soaked uniform was on the floor. He sat down on a bench and looked up at Drover.

"You were never into it. You did something in high school? Football?"

"Basketball."

"Nothin' in college."

"Too short. White men can't jump."

"That's a fact," Homer said. "Me, I was a baseball player. All I ever was, all I ever wanted to be. Didn't give a rat's ass for nothin' else. When I was a kid, go down by the rail yards and hit cans and stones with a stick. Throw 'em up in the air and hit 'em a lick. Didn't matter if no one was around, did it for myself. Liked to feel that, hittin' a can, send that sucker up flyin'. Used to hit cans against the coal cars, thinkin' the sides of the cars was baseball-field fences. You know? I could take that stick and let the old boy throw as hard as he could against me and I knew I'd tan it three or four times out of ten. That means I knew what it was I wanted to do all my life. You maybe knew what you wanted to do, maybe not. I knew. Man, there is nothing sweeter than the smell of a ballpark. There is nothing like the cheers of the fans. Nothing like standing there with the stick and looking at that fat piece of shit sixtyfeetsix away and know, *know* in your heart that tonight you are going to knock that ball to hell and gone."

He shook his head. He stared at the floor, stared at his own scarred white legs.

"Now look at me. I got to live with these legs but these legs ain't gonna finish Homer A. White. Almighty God invented the Designated Hitter rule for me. I have been Chosen, Brother Drover. I am not mocking the Lord now, don't think that. But there it is. I am a DH, and if I can get through this season without pills, if I can play through the pain, I can show the AL that one of them ought to be paying me a million and a half a year for my hitting talents. I gotta go .290 or thereabouts and I gotta go thirty-three or thirty-four and I gotta go a hundred ribbies. Then I can walk out of goddamned Wrigley Field and Eddie Briggs and tell them to stick it up their ass."

"Eddie Briggs? The general manager? What's it with Eddie Briggs?"

"Eddie Briggs is a piece of shit."

"All GMs are. They're paid to be. But what is your problem with him specifically?"

"Look, Drover, you ain't even supposed to be in this locker room. Why don't you get the fuck out of my life before I throw you out?"

"I don't fight with cripples."

Homer grabbed a bat in his stall and threw it, but Drover put up his hands and ducked. The bat splashed into the water of the whirlpool tub. Homer was on his feet, pain or no pain, and he was at Drover just as he delivered the first punch.

It hurt, and Drover took a second one before he could deliver his first. They did a baseball sort of fight after that, falling to the floor and rolling around. The only way they could have hurt each other was by bumping into furniture.

"All right," Drover said, all out of breath.

"All right?"

"All right. We got to break this up before the team comes back or they'll think we're married."

"You take that back."

"I just wanted to crack you one. I take it back."

" 'Cause I ain't no cripple. Maybe I will be if this goes on and gets worse, but right now I ain't no cripple."

"You ain't no cripple," Drover said.

"I said I ain't no fucking cripple," Homer said.

They were both gasping for breath.

"Say it," Homer said.

"I said it already," Drover said.

"You son of a bitch."

Drover held on to the man because he thought if he let Homer go, Homer would explode again and start the fight all over. He felt the naked back heave. And then he realized what was going on when Homer said it again about not being a cripple. For Christ's sake, he was crying.

Drover disengaged then. Slowly. He got up from the floor and turned away. Homer was lying on the floor and he was crying, but now he was trying to snuff it up and he made snuffling noises.

A minute or two passed. Drover kept staring at the whirlpool so he wouldn't have to look at Homer White. When he started to speak again, his back was still turned away.

"Your wife. Mae. She talked to me. She wanted to talk about you. She said you were hurting and that a guy wanted you in Seattle but the Cubs wouldn't make a deal. You think that's true?"

"You're the last person I would have asked her to talk to. I don't know why the hell she did it."

"You see her?"

"After the accident. Came down to see if I was dead. I wasn't dead so she went back to Seattle."

"That the only time?"

"Only time."

"That was a long time ago. Before you got your arthritis." Drover turned now and the man wasn't crying. He was sitting in his stall, a towel wrapped around his private parts, his forearms on his thighs. But he was looking at Drover.

"Maybe I talked to her one more time. We talked about the kid. Kid needed some money so I sent her some."

"What was her name? Millie?"

"Yeah. I didn't do right by the kid. Helen tells me that and she's right."

"Who's Helen?"

"When I was in therapy after the accident I met a fine lady named Helen. Worked in the rehab institute. Thass all."

"And she told you you didn't treat your kid right?"

"She told me a lot of things about myself. Made me stand up to myself. To the bad things."

"You told Mae you were hurting."

"I mentioned it when she started on about my career being over because I was hitting so bad last season. She didn't know a damn thing. I was still takin' the pills for the arthritis and I couldn't hit a lick. Gonna live with the pain this time. I can still hit, can't I, Drover? Punched that sorry-ass son of a bitch for two tonight."

"You got the eye still."

"I ain't got the wheels but if I handle it this year, I can go to anyone in the AL."

"You'd have to sit out a year—you got a contract."

"Ah can't sit out no year. You sit out a year, you lost a year out of your life. Lord only gives a ballplayer so many years and you can't spend 'em messin' around sittin' out."

"Why does Eddie Briggs hold on to you?"

"Because he's a pissant."

"Aside from that."

"How the hell do I know? I just know. I talked to him even before spring training and he just smiled at me and said it must feel weird for me to be held by the nuts now for a change. Crazy son of a bitch."

"You have a good year, Homer, Cubs could get a good trade for you. Right now, you're semi-worthless to anyone in the AL."

"I know."

Drover was thinking about it. "What if someone, a part owner, wants you for a team but he's got to convince other people you're worth something, that you haven't lost it. I see it now. It makes sense in parts. Max Heubner may want you but he can't get you until he can get some toehold on Briggs on the Cubs."

"I don't know what you're talking about. In fact, I don' wanna talk to you no more. Not tonight or never. Get out of my life, willya?"

Drover nodded then. "OK, Homer."

He took a step toward the door. He turned. In the corner, a TV monitor was scanning the remains of the game. The Cubs were wrapping it up.

"I'm sorry for your trouble, Homer," Drover said. It was the last thing he ever thought he'd say.

NINE

DROVER WENT home to Santa Cruz by way of Vegas.

The city that the mob built is not nearly as bright at night as people say it is. It is merely that the desert all around is so dark. McCarran International sits just a few miles south of downtown and a stone's throw from the glitter of the Strip, formally Las Vegas Boulevard. It is a city of commerce, burnout, high hopes, deep despairs, and organized sleaze. Drover always thought that if there really is a hell, it is probably a lot like Las Vegas: There are no clocks and you have to keep pulling slots for all eternity.

It was time to make up with Fox Vernon and see what this was really all about. The sight of Homer White crying in the locker room had rattled his cage full of careful grudges and prejudices. Drover never could kick a man when he was down, which explained his lack of a killer instinct.

Fox Vernon was alive at midnight because the day was in its infancy for him. Like nearly everyone connected with the world's biggest gambling center, Vernon easily mixed up days and nights.

His oddsmaking enterprise operated in a separate building behind the Shamrock Casino Hotel on the Strip. It was a sober place full of sober young men and women who crunched numbers in computers to learn the truth of them. Sort of like chasing neutrons in an atomic accelerator lab. And about as exciting. When you can reduce sports down to numbers, it loses a lot of its fascination.

Drover passed himself into the offices and waited for Foxy to let him enter the sanctum. Fox saw him but let him wait. When he pushed the buzzer releasing the door lock, two minutes had passed. Not that you'd find a clock in the town to measure it by.

"Are you done being mad at me?" Fox Vernon asked. His voice was mild, filtered for feeling the way the air in the windowless room was filtered. One of the Vegas stories is that you find the strength to stay up all night and gamble because the drinks are watered and raw oxygen is pumped constantly into the smoke-filled casinos. Both elements of the story are true.

"Not yet," Drover said. He took a pew and filled it with his frame. Vernon sat behind his desk in front of a blinking computer screen. "The guy I was supposed to do dirt on is Homer White."

"He hit two tonight," Fox Vernon said.

"I was there."

"And?"

"And nothing. This thing is goofy if you're telling me the truth," Drover said.

"I told you I don't lie."

"Then his ex-wife and a general partner in the Mariners as well as Elmore Leonardo and some other creep I don't know yet are all yin-and-yanging Homer White for reasons too obscure for me. The wife says the general partner wants to hire on Homer as a DH because DH's don't need wheels and Homer is losing his legs. That part about losing his legs is real. Homer said he had a rotten year last year because of his medication for the arthritis that attacked his legs after his accident. Now he is, as they say, playing with pain to prove that he can still hit."

Fox hit a few buttons on the computer keyboard. He spoke in that same colorless—even diffident—voice that admits to no sports enthusiasm at all.

"Hitting .345 the first two weeks. Eight homers counting tonight. He's going to be a cover boy on SI before long."

"Not that racist redneck sonofabitch."

"You don't like him," Fox said.

Drover said nothing. He thought of a naked man crying. And he didn't want to think about him that way.

"You know I checked him out over those gambling rumors. I said he was clean. I still think he's clean. I think someone or maybe a bunch of people are setting him up but I can't figure out who or for what reason. Everyone seems on a different side."

"There are things I don't like about the game of baseball," Fox Vernon began. He was staring at his computer screen. Every now and then, his fingers would flick over the keyboard, punch this letter and that, and new images would fill the screen. None of it interrupted his monologue.

"I don't like what was done to the last commissioner. I don't like salary arbitration because it encourages disloyalty and allows teams to overload the payroll. I don't like the reliance on television money because TV is going to figure out finally that baseball is not a television game, not at the level the networks expect it to be. And I don't like organized greed on any level. The owners are out of control. Do you know how many there are? Twenty-eight franchises in the Bigs. There are something like four hundred people who can walk around and say they own a piece of this team or that. It's nice on the ego for them but bad on the paperwork for me."

"So you heard a rumor that maybe Max Heubner wanted to buy Homer White," Drover guessed.

Vernon nodded at his screen. "Heard it a couple of weeks ago. And then along comes Elmore Leonardo saying he had to desperately get in touch with you in Seattle. He knew you were somewhere in Seattle. How did he know that?"

Drover shrugged.

"Well, your life is an open book," Vernon said. "Maybe you said something once to someone about where you go to finish up books. But it was the emphasis that Elmore put on it. Seattle. He wanted to see you in Seattle, something he knew about baseball, something you'd want to know. What did I connect it to? That I heard Seattle might be interested in Homer White. And then I connected it back to . . . to your trouble ten years ago. Didn't Homer White give a deposition? Sure he did. We must have talked about it once. So I gave your address to Elmore because I wanted to see if all these things connected."

"And you were testing me again," Drover said.

"Maybe," Fox Vernon said.

"I was never in the Outfit," Drover said.

"I believe you."

"But what the hell, it's just a test, as the teachers say," Drover said.

Fox Vernon looked away from the screen.

For a moment, they stared at each other.

"Let's say you connected all the dots," Fox said. "Heubner. Elmore. Homer White."

"Why, you're as sly as a Fox," Drover said. "You're using the Socratic method as it applies to the way I live my life. You want me to find my own way to your conclusion."

"That isn't quite what Socrates was about," Vernon said.

"Max Heubner is involved with the wise guys."

"Maybe," Fox Vernon said. "On the surface, it could look that way. Elmore wants to give you dirt on Homer and the next thing you know, Heubner—"

"He sent his girlfriend to me. Who happens to be Homer White's ex-wife."

"And he's using Homer's ex-wife to . . . I'm getting lost."

Drover said, "I am in Seattle, minding my own business. Elmore Leonardo and another guy take me for a short ride and give me an envelope full of dirt on Homer White. A picture of him with a Chicago mobster and some Xerox copies of betting slips that might belong to Homer White. Except you know what betting slips are. If these are real, which I doubt. They also booga-booga me. They want me to plant them with some newspaper writers to put heat on the commissioner, who would then put heat on Homer. The next day, I get a call from Mae Tilson, who is living in Seattle and used to be Homer's wife. She buys me dinner and says she's been talking to Homer and that the Cubs' GM won't sell his contract to Max Heubner of Seattle.

And Max Heubner is her ex-squeeze. I know. That's the *Soap Opera Digest* version but I don't know where it goes from there."

"Why won't Eddie Briggs of Chicago surrender Homer White to Seattle? I mean, it's not as though they have to play Seattle unless the impossible ever happens and the Mariners and the Cubs find themselves in the same World Series."

"CBS would love that. Chicago and Seattle. What a matchup," Drover said.

"The Cubs would need a left fielder," Fox said, "but left fielders are more dime-a-dozen guys than finding a long reliever. The Cubs could free up six million over the next four years to buy some youth. Eddie Briggs is a youth guy, always was, every team he was at. He's at the Cubs less than a year, he didn't sign Homer White's last contract, he doesn't usually want to hang on to over-the-hillers."

"Homer doesn't like him."

Fox punched a button and turned off the screen. He flicked a switch on the side of the set and shut off the computer. He sat for a moment, contemplating the death of the program he was working on. Then he got up from his chair and walked around the desk with the distracted air of a college professor lecturing on abstract ideals.

"Homer White could be faking his pain. Don't interrupt. Homer and his ex-wife could be tied into this with Heubner. Don't ask me how or why, I'm trying to follow a thought. The element I don't like is Elmore Leonardo wanting to give you incriminations about Homer White and bringing along some mysterious other to enforce it. You had already been over that ground this winter so why would you do it again? And why you?"

He stopped, stared at the only pupil in the lecture hall, and continued:

"Because you had animus toward Homer White because of something that happened ten years ago. Something Elmore knew about. Is it striking you about now that this is an extraordinarily tangled web weaving around one worthless and washed-up old ballplayer whose contract, however personally lucrative, is ho-hum by baseball standards?"

"Yes."

"Good. I was afraid I was the only one."

"You forgot something. You were dragged into this too, by the fact that Elmore involved you in looking for me while I was finishing your book in Seattle."

"No. I would have gotten to it. Are we being set up, James?" Foxy never called him James unless he was terribly upset. "Is Homer? Is some dark and dastardly deed being done in the Bigs by one of its four hundred or so part-time owners?"

"Max Heubner."

"The core of the problem, I think," Fox said.

Drover blinked more than once in the strong, postmidnight fluorescent lighting. Maybe it was the blinks that did it.

Because he saw it too. Not the answer or anything close to it. Just the core of the problem.

TEN

Max Heubner ate a salad for breakfast. He took care of himself, and this was one of the odd ways he did it. He was fifty-five and didn't look it. He had big hands and they had been all over Mae Tilson for hours during the night. She was sleeping in his big bed and he was eating a salad with a glass of skim milk in the kitchen.

He had built the house. It was six thousand square feet of ostentation. He had built the house when he had a wife and two kids. He still had the two kids, of course, but they were long gone from the nest. The ex-wife was living back in her childhood hometown, Portland. He never saw her and never wanted to see her again.

Mae was thirty-seven and fucked like twenty-one. Max knew. He had tried going the twenty-one route a few times but they were so fucking stupid. They knew how to fuck but they didn't know anything else. Max liked to talk to someone sometimes.

When he finished his salad, he took the plate and put it in the sink. He was very neat, which made living in a six-thousand-square-foot house possible. The maid came five mornings a week and did everything else, including tearing up lettuce for his evening salad and the next morning's salad. Max tried to eat fruits and vegetables in excess.

Mae wore a silver satin nightgown with thin straps and a long leg slit. She looked like a million dollars to Max, even at seven in the morning. She shuffled into the kitchen in her slippers and opened the refrigerator.

Max had finished reading the *Seattle Post-Intelligencer* and was working on *The Wall Street Journal.* He was drinking tea now and neither of them spoke to the other while Mae rummaged through the refrigerator. She found a bottle of Perrier water and removed it. Then she rummaged through a drawer for an opener. Then she rummaged through a cabinet for a glass. All her movements were sleepwalking.

She kissed him on the forehead before she sat down across from him.

There was a fog on the trees beyond the windows of the kitchen. The fog pressed against the glass and diffused the light.

She drank some of the bubbly water.

"There's tea," he said, his eyes on the paper.

"I hate tea. Why don't you get a coffeemaker."

"Coffee'll kill you."

"Everything will kill you eventually."

"I read an article that people could live to be four hundred."

"God, I'd hate that. Four hundred. Four hundred Christmases. God, I'd hate that," Mae said. She was gradually waking up. She glanced at the front page of the *Post-Intelligencer.* She made out the words.

He put down his paper and looked at her. "Like we talked about last night, Mae."

"I know, I know," she said.

"Well, I have to press you a little."

"I know," she said. "I'll call him today."

"This morning," he said.

"What's the rush, anyway? You never tell me everything."

"I never tell anyone everything," Max said.

"That's true, Max. It doesn't make you very trustworthy."

"I'm trustworthy," Max said. "I want you to call him this morning. We got to get off the pot on this. You should never have walked out on him Sunday night. I set that up careful and you fucked it up."

"I fucked it up? He was an asshole."

"And then you go and tell him everything you know about him and what good does that do, to tell him all that shit?" Max said it and then glowered at her.

She glowered back. She put down her glass of bubbly water and said, "Why don't you just have him killed?"

"Drover?"

"You know who I mean."

"I can't arrange that."

"I thought you could arrange everything."

"I can arrange everything here, not there. There's different territories involved in this. Chicago is not a town where you go in from outside and get someone killed. Everyone is connected there and they don't like freelance killings. You go in the right way and clear it with them, then they know your business and they want a piece of it. No, Mae. I can't kill him in Chicago."

"You know those people. Why don't you just tell one of them to arrange it."

"That would be terrific, Mae, it really would. Just kill him. Just kill a major league baseball player like that. That's terrific thinking, Mae. Sometimes I don't think you follow through because you get so mad about something, like you did with that Drover guy the other night. What were you thinking? The answer is: You weren't. You just got on your high horse and rode off. So now what? We got to go over this again."

"You don't just kill him. A car hits him. He's shown he's accident prone. You could have him have a heart attack. Or fall in the bathroom. People are always falling in bathrooms, aren't they? He's not in the best of shape. Going to that therapist, that fucking bitch, that fucking bitch."

"Take it easy, Mae."

"I'm not gonna take it easy. His money belongs to me. Me and Millicent."

"And you're going to get it, Mae. We're going to get it."

"And then we get married and sign the contract."

"Then we get married and we sign the contract."

"I'm not ever going to be fucked around by a man again. Not him and not you, Max."

"Honey, I'm not going to screw you."

"I hate that word. Just so you know, Max, I really have had it with being fucked by men."

"You haven't had it with me, have you? I mean, you still like to do it." He tried a smile now because Mae's temperature was up about three thousand degrees.

Mae just stared at him but he saw she was cooling down and the color was draining from her lovely cheeks. She was so pretty in all her parts, he would think, and then when she got mad, he would think that he was nearly afraid of her.

When she spoke again, her voice was calm. "This seems so complicated to me."

"We have to do it this way."

"Tell me again."

"Mae."

"Tell me again."

"Mae, Mae. We all want something in this world, right? You want something, I want something, they want something. So when you and I first met, you want something from me and I want you. I still want you."

"Yes."

"It's simple. You want Homer's money. He's got a trust fund for Millicent, but if he dies suddenly he leaves it all to Millie. So you try it on your own and you nearly screw it up, getting that pickup truck fixed on him. If I'd known you better then, I could have arranged that."

"But you can't arrange to kill him in Chicago."

"Honey, you can't just shoot down a major league baseball player. It's like shooting a president."

"What's the big deal about that? We do that all the time."

"Honey, listen to me. This is a better way. Get him out of baseball, out of the spotlight. Then we do it to him. We can get him run down by a car or something in Arkansas but you can't arrange shit like that in Chicago with the kind of people I deal with."

"With the Mafia."

"Eh, Mafia. Let us say, people who work together. The Mafia thing I'm not comfortable with. They have been good to me. They've put money into the things I do. They've built this house, for Christ's sake. They're investors like investors anywhere. But when it comes down to it, they're hard-headed businessmen too. They want return. Some of my . . . own investments aren't so hot."

"You could ask them to do a simple thing, just kill Homer."

"I ask them that, what do they ask of me? They ask me the next time to do what? Fix a game for them, for Christ's sake? I'm not getting involved in that shit, I'd be up to my ass in alligators with that shit. I just ask a little favor, a little screen action they don't even know what it is. Pass on some rumors to this Drover guy that Homer is gambling, hanging out with the Outfit. Give him a photo of a certain Chicago guy sitting with Homer. You know, insinuation. Maybe this will get an investigation, maybe it will get him banned from baseball. It's a long shot but a shot. In the meantime, I tell you to let Homer know and to let this Drover know that I want our team to buy Homer's contract. It's a second ploy. You never let one hand know what the other hand is doing."

"You're driving me crazy."

"Mae, you got to listen, you got to be patient. I been talking to our GM about Homer and he's not crazy about him. I bring his name up at a partnership meeting and what do I get but stares. But I am patient. You don't build a development overnight. You take time, you drop a hint, you arrange a meet, you pick up a tab, you do the little things, you just keep nudging it along."

"And meanwhile, he is fucking around with that fucking bitch. He told me, 'Mae, I never thought I would get married again, I never thought I was ever going to be in love again, least of all with someone like her, but I love her, I honest to God love her.' " She made a face. "That stupid son of a bitch is going to go get married and I am going to lose everything."

"Millicent still gets the trust fund."

"It's the same difference. Millicent will do exactly what I tell her to do, the fucked-up little bitch."

Her cheeks were blushing again and Max thought that was a bad sign. He saw Mae go off, sometimes three or four times a day, just fly off the handle about something. No wonder she couldn't keep a secretary in her office. He wouldn't put up with it himself. She had slapped him once and he had beaten her up, just like that; she couldn't go out for a week because of her black eyes. But then it had settled down between them. Because she wanted something and he wanted something.

She wanted those three hundred acres outside of Caswell. So did he. Three hundred acres off County XX. The Japanese were building a car plant in Caswell not two miles from those three hundred beautiful wooded acres where Homer White had his house. Given this and that, he could develop that into fifteen million dollars for himself and fifteen for his business partners and, of course, money for Mae, a lot more money than she had ever seen in her life.

"Honey," he said. "You got to control yourself. He hasn't married this Helen Brown. He wouldn't have met Helen Brown if you hadn't screwed up on the pickup truck."

"I didn't screw up, that dopey shit I hired screwed up. Women are always being fucked around by men. Like you're fucking me around now. Do this, do that, be careful, make me take all the risks, make me go to this Drover geek and pass on the story—"

"He knows I can't talk to him. He's sort of in a twilight zone when it comes to sports. An owner can't be talking to someone who works for gamblers."

"Like the gamblers you know."

"I never been in Vegas, I am very clean. What I do in my business life is always under scrutiny, but they can't make any connections. You know why I like being a part owner in baseball? Because it means those guys have to keep their distance from me. I like them being careful, it makes my life easier. Everyone treats a baseball owner with respect, even if I only have five percent."

"I just say you could have him killed."

"No. Never step outside your role in life with those people. For those people, I am a conduit of profits for their laundry. They give me money and I build things and you sell these things and you make money, I make money, and my investors make money, all of it legitimate money. That's the way to do things. Keep it simple."

"Killing Homer is simple."

"Homer will be killed one way or another in time. I get him in Seattle, I can have him whacked. I get him kicked out of baseball, I can have him whacked in Arkansas. He becomes an ex-jock, he fades from the spotlight and we can get it done. Besides, he comes to Seattle, he won't be seeing his Chicago girl. He'll be under your influence again, Mae. You can see him as much as you want."

"I never had a problem with men. I could use them well. Except Homer had this other thing. This fucking game he played. Stupid fucking baseball. He'd talk about it all the time, it drove me crazy. Everything was about the game, the edge he had, the way he'd do sit-ups or push-ups when I was waiting for him in bed. Stupid bastard," she said.

"It made him great," he said.

"You know what's going to happen, don't you? He's going to sell that property in Caswell and go live in Chicago with her. She won't ever go down home," Mae Tilson said.

"Mae, honey, they aren't married. Homer is telling you he's in love but apparently she isn't in love with him."

"That bitch—Homer is a meal ticket for her, she'll marry him, she's just stringing him."

"Mae, be patient. Make the call this morning. Do what I'm telling you." He touched her gently on her faintly glowing cheek. He smiled at her. "Come on, Mae."

She let herself smile then. She kissed the palm of his outstretched hand.

They got up from the kitchen table. They kept touching. They kissed each other.

This was the way it was supposed to be, he thought.

It must be all those salads.

ELEVEN

Drover slept in one of the comp rooms at the Shamrock until nearly nine the next morning. His flight to SFX would leave at eleven, which gave him enough time for the shower-and-shave routine as well as a typical casino breakfast. You may lose all your money in Vegas but you can't lose weight there. For a few bucks, breakfast buffets all over town stretch from this end of the table to way over there.

His first pleasant surprise of the day was at McCarren airport.

He and Lori Gibbons were booked on the same plane.

Lori was an attendant for United, a woman with classical features that reminded many people of Lee Remick. She was statuesque in looks and manners. She said that she enjoyed being in the airline business, but in her next life, she might be a brain surgeon. The funny thing was that it was perfectly believable.

They had met a couple of years ago when she was the girlfriend of a Denver Bronco quarterback. That was long over, and it wasn't that she and Drover were steadies, but they kept going to other people and coming back to each other. The last few months had been Lori's turn to go to other people.

"I think this is fate," she said, settling in next to him in first class. The plane was half full and Lori was grabbing a free ride to SFX. She was in mufti, which today meant corduroy slacks and a sweater.

"You just don't seem like the kind of girl who'd be found in Vegas. In fact, I remember you lecturing me once on the evils of gambling."

"I never did. If I thought it was evil, I wouldn't speak to you," she said. She smiled and the world smiled back at her.

The plane kicked off the rhumba line and leaped down the runway like a dancer crossing the stage in a ballet. It was very graceful, and they rose quickly over the city and then across the desert reaches glittering under the sun, dead and dried and full of bones.

"What I said was that gambling was something I could take or leave," she continued.

"So you were taking," he said.

"No. One of the girls quit to have babies. She lives in Boulder. I was visiting her for the day. I've got a week's furlough and nothing to do with it. Actually, I might have been thinking about going down to Santa Cruz to see Nancy and Kelly."

"And me?"

"Well, it's been a while. Are you engaged or anything since I last saw you?"

"You know you're the only girl for me."

"If that were true, we'd have problems," Lori said.

"I don't know why you want to play the field when I'm in the game."

"Is that a sports metaphor?" she asked.

"I try them out now and then so they won't creep up in my writing."

"Have you been writing?"

"I took a couple of weeks of retreat in Seattle."

"Seattle?"

"Would you like to go to Seattle with me? I mean, maybe tomorrow?"

"What's in Seattle?"

"Starbucks coffee. The Public Market. The Space Needle. The tallest building west of Chicago. Puget Sound ferries. Rain."

She slipped her hand into his hand. The seat belt lights went out and the pilot came on to do two minutes of Chuck Yeager. When he was finished, Drover said, "I have to see a man there. It's a brief errand and it won't be pleasant, but afterwards we can pretend."

"Pretend what?"

"Anything you want."

"Is everything all right?"

"I guess so. A funny thing came up last weekend in Seattle. I was there finishing the football book."

"I was in Seattle. I mean, a week ago. I was substituting on the Seattle-Chicago run."

"Damn, why didn't you tell me?"

"Why didn't you tell me?" she said.

"Does it ever seem to you that we are ships passing in the night too often?"

"I don't know, Jim." Her mouth turned down. The sun above the clouds seemed to darken. She had that effect on weather. "You're awfully mixed up and you never seem to get unmixed, you know? You're nearly middle-aged and you still don't know what you want to be when you grow up."

"A great writer. I decided that in Seattle doing the football book. I want to write something like *War and Peace*."

"About Vietnam."

"No. Bigger than that. No one wants to read one more burned-out account of Vietnam. Besides, kids think Vietnam was something that happened right around the Civil War. No, I want to write a book about a man obsessed with writing *War and Peace* without ever realizing that it has already been written."

Lori said, "I don't understand that at all."

"Sort of a meditation on the absurdity of wanting to be a great writer," Drover said.

"Are you being deep or silly?"

He glanced out the window. Sunlight above the clouds. "I want to get some perspective on what it is I want to be if I grow up. I was thinking this morning about someone. He's in sports, he plays a child's game for a living."

"In football."

"Baseball. Football is understandable. It really isn't a child's game, it's chess for crazy people who like to hit each other. Football players, I mean, and everyone who likes watching football. But baseball is theater of the absurd. You get people like George Will, this big commentator, writing about the profundity of baseball. What a crock, but there's a book like that being published all the time. Shit between covers."

"I don't like that word."

"Sorry. This guy, this ballplayer, has screwed up his whole life during his whole life and then, one dark and stormy night in Georgia, although it was really Arkansas, he's in a terrible car accident and breaks his legs. His legs heal but he develops arthritis in the healed joints and now he's coming to the end of his career and he refuses to accept it. You know what that is? It's a metaphor for death. And that explains wanting to become a great writer."

"I don't get it."

"I don't either." He seemed to be coming out of something. He suddenly smiled at her. "We'll take a limo down to Cruz and eat pot roast with Kelly and Nancy. Today is always pot roast day. Pot roast and boiled potatoes and carrots."

"I don't know why I love that man's food so much."

"Because it's the food of our people. Common people's food. It makes us children again," Drover said.

"You're full of it today, Jim."

"I usually suppress it but I'm full of it every day. Do you ever think that buildings downtown get lonely when all the people go away for the weekend?"

"Sure," she said. Just like that. He wanted to kiss her then, but he didn't want to embarrass her. He held off. The plane sailed into California and began to descend through the clouds.

TWELVE

KELLY SERVED up his famous pot roast with a flourish that was Julia Child in exuberance without a trace of the smarminess of the Frugal Gourmet. Besides, you could believe Julia would enjoy pot roast but that the Frug would find a way to turn it into a cross-cultural experience.

The joint was jumping for a Tuesday. Toby took the regulars at the bar and Sanchez was laboring in a hot kitchen. Nancy was up and down at her hostessing job but Kelly acted as if all the hubbub of the world he had created around him did not exist.

Lori Gibbons used her knife and fork like the trencherwoman she was. Beneath that size six beat the heart of a real fattie. They drank Old Style beer, imported by Kelly from Chicago, and swabbed the gravy up with pieces of French bread.

Halfway through, Drover said, "We're going up to Seattle tomorrow. I want to see a guy there. Lori said she'd show me the sights. I didn't see them the last time I was there."

"Seattle," Kelly said. He interrupted himself to spread another dab of horseradish on the pot roast. "I got a call this morning for you. From a Mae Tilson in Seattle. Is that the woman you talked to last time?"

Lori stared at the piece of pot roast at the end of her fork. It was an interesting piece of pot roast. She brought it to her lips, opened her mouth, and took it inside.

"Homer White's ex-wife," Drover said. To Kelly. To Lori Gibbons. "Where are these people getting all these phone numbers? I'm not listed."

"They called me. In the bar."

"Who the hell are these people anyway? They reach me in Seattle, they call you for me. Damn." He put down his fork just a little too hard and they both noticed.

Lori said. "Who is she?"

"She's Homer White's ex-wife. He's a baseball player. On the Cubs. The one I was metaphoring about on the plane. She called me in Seattle. We had dinner and she gives me some story . . . well, it's complicated, Lori, I'll tell you about it on the way up."

"Maybe I shouldn't go. I don't want to interfere with whatever you have to do up there."

"Believe me, Lori, you're not interfering, you're my lifeline to sanity. You know, Kelly, I don't even like baseball that much. Why is this coming down on me?"

"You're the designated hitter," Kelly said. "You only do one thing well, which is to nose around in the wide world of sports and find out the truth of things. So all kinds of people use you for this one thing."

"What's a designated hitter?" Lori said. Baseball was not her game.

Kelly told her and gave her his opinion of designated hitters in general and the rule that had created the position in the American League twenty years earlier.

"Baseball is a sacred game of sacred traditions and they shouldn't have messed with it," Kelly ended.

"You like baseball?"

"I liked going to Wrigley Field when I was a kid," Kelly said.

"You never have a baseball game on TV here unless someone asks for it," Drover said.

"It bores me on TV," Kelly said. "Baseball is a game for the fresh air, in daylight, the way the Cubs used to always play it. Popcorn. Beer. Sit back, make bets, relax. You don't get that on TV. Besides, I'm in northern California now and we don't do baseball here."

"That would come as a surprise to the Oakland A's," Drover said.

"Oakland is in its own world," Kelly said. "It has nothing to do with California. Baseball in San Francisco is just another tourist attraction. It's not *soul* up here. Anyway, this Mae person said you should call her because it was important. Not urgent or I would have told you right away. It was important."

"You balanced that in your mind and thought your pot roast was more important. At least more urgent," Drover said.

Kelly growled a laugh that time. He was a big man and ate with knife and fork in the European way. The pot roast and the potatoes did not stand a chance. "I got the number behind the bar."

They ate on.

"What can I do for you?" Drover said. The telephone in his apartment was in the bedroom. Lori and Kelly and Nancy were in the bar, deep in old-home-week stuff. None of them had family and so they were becoming their own made-up family. Dan Quayle would not have approved.

"I want to apologize first."

"Forget it. It was a good meal."

"Still."

"Forget it."

"Really. Sometimes I get carried away."

"Forget it," Drover said a third time.

There was a pause while they forgot it.

"All right. I want to tell you what I was going to tell you."

"Back up. First, are you still going with Max Heubner?"

"I told you. We're just friends. And we do business from time to time."

"I want to get hold of him. You got numbers for him?"

"I told you, he can't see you, you're a gambler—"

"And I told you I wasn't. It doesn't matter. I have to see him. You got numbers for him?"

A long pause.

He waited, staring at the blank notepad on the nightstand by the bed.

"What do you want to see him about?" she said finally.

"That's between us," Drover said.

"He won't see you."

"You'd be surprised how many people say that to me and don't really mean it."

"He can't. He doesn't want to . . . be involved—"

"Listen, Mae. He's involved because he's involved me. In a lot of ways. I didn't go to Seattle to visit with anybody, but by God, a lot of people, including you, wanted to visit with me. Tell me, Mae, how do you know so much about me, right down to my phone numbers?"

"I told you. Max. He wanted— He said he wanted me to— Well, I was involved. I mean, with Homer. Homer said." None of it was coming out in the right way and she was stopping, trying to start over again.

"You said, he said. What is it that I have to find out about Eddie Briggs? Stop Socratizing me."

"I don't know about that," she said. "I just know he won't sell Homer's contract to Max and Max wants it and Homer wants it."

"Homer says he doesn't know anything about Max."

That got her.

Long pause this time.

Then: "You talked to him."

"I talked to him."

"You talked to him about me?"

"Some."

"What did he say?"

"He said you talked to him about sending money to Millie. He said he did."

"Well, he did. I mean, I did."

"He said he doesn't know anything about Seattle."

"Well, that's a lie. That's Homer, he's a fucking liar." Just like that, she was off the handle. They waited for her to return.

"I mean, why would he lie to you?" she said.

Drover waited.

She said, "I'm doing this for him. He wants to get out of the

National League so bad. You saw him. You saw he's crippled up."

"He isn't a cripple. In fact, he looked pretty good. He's just hit two home runs against the Rockies. We talked a lot about old times. We used to party on Division and Rush streets when we were younger. Did you know that?"

"Some."

"He must have been married to you around then. Or recently married to you. Well, that was the old days. Anyway, he says he loves the Cubs now and everything is hunky and I must say, it looks good. He's hitting their socks off. I mean, eight home runs in fourteen games is phenomenal."

Drover was trying to sound like a cheerful idiot. It worked.

She sputtered now. "That's just not true."

"It is true. I saw it with my own eyeballs. He hit two off a kid who is probably contemplating a long bus trip down to Nebraska right now."

"I mean, I know that. I mean, I know he's been hitting. But we . . . we were talking about Seattle. I've talked to him about Seattle. About what Max wants him to do."

"Well, maybe Homer doesn't want to do what Max wants him to do."

Bingo.

She didn't say anything for ten seconds. That is a long time on long distance.

And then she let it go.

"Did he mention his girlfriend?"

"Girlfriend?"

"Nothing."

"Nothing?"

"No, I was thinking of something else," she said.

"What girlfriend? What's that got to do with anything?" Drover closed his eyes, trying to recall the conversation in the locker room, trying to remember anything Rusty had said. Anything Mae had said in that Italian restaurant outside Seattle on Sunday night.

Girlfriend?

"Hello," she said. "Are you still there?"

"I'm still here."

"Anyway, I wish you'd let me see you. Talk to you about—"

"Oh, Christ, I don't want to talk to you about Homer White or Eddie Briggs. Eddie Briggs might have a lot of good reasons for hanging on to Homer right now. His price goes up every time he hits a goner and he's been hitting them the first fourteen games. Maybe Eddie Briggs shopped him last season and didn't get any takers because he was playing so bad. Maybe Max Heubner wants to get him cheap, make the Cubs pay part of the rest of his contract in exchange for Seattle taking him off its hands. All kinds of crazy deals go down in baseball. I'm not even interested in that. Baseball is so complicated now that I might as well spend my life translating Dead Sea Scrolls."

"I don't understand that."

"Neither do I. Just put it this way. I would love to see you again for any reason other than to talk about Homer White, but because that is all you would talk about, I give up on the pleasure of your company. Could you please give me some numbers for Max Heubner?"

"I mean, if you don't want to talk about Homer, why are you bothering Max?"

"It's my secret."

"Please." Soft now. "I want to see you. I really do." Very soft. "I promise I won't talk about Homer, I promise. I just want to see you. We can go back to Luigi's. I promise I'll be good."

Oh, God.

It went on like this for another thirty seconds.

Finally, Drover broke the connection without speaking. He sat on the edge of his bed for a long time. Mae was going to tell Max and what would Max do? Call up the goon patrol he had put on Drover in the first place? Leonardo and his buddy? This was a variation on good cop–bad cop and the variation was that one set of guys wanted him to get Homer and, if that didn't work, the other set wanted him to save Homer. Why me? Drover said to himself again. And then thought of Kelly in the bar. The designated hitter. Because that was the one thing he did well.

THIRTEEN

THE CUBS flew back to Chicago on Tuesday night after a day game with the Rockies. Denver put that one away in the eighth with a bases-loaded homer highlighting a nine-run laugher of an inning. Baseball is a long season and even the best of teams—the one that wins the World Series in the fall—can count on losing a third of its games just by the nature and length of the season.

The terrible, absolutely horrible, and very bad eighth inning had been too much.

Homer White chased balls all over the outfield that inning and just stood there while fourteen Rockies trooped to the plate. It just about killed his legs. The damned inning lasted nearly fifty minutes. One damned inning. He was so disgusted, all he had wanted to do was shower and get the hell out of there. The plane took off at seven and touched down at O'Hare in Chicago shortly after 1:00 A.M.

It was nearly two when he got to the apartment he rented in a condo high rise in Streeterville downtown. The city lights were all on and he could see the black lake out his window, rippling in the moonlight. He turned on the Jacuzzi in his bathroom and climbed in and fell asleep as the warm water stroked his aching legs.

In his dream, the same old dream, he was driving the old pickup up Double X to the farm and he was going faster and faster, laughing all the way. Only in the dream, Helen Brown was next to him on the bench seat and she was saying over and over that he was going too fast and he was laughing at her and saying she was chicken and then, when he made the turn onto the pea gravel, the truck flipped and she was thrown right through the windshield. In the dream, he could move and he climbed out of the truck and she was lying on the grass in the rain and she looked like a broken doll.

He woke up saying strange things. Never words he recognized. He once asked Helen if he was speaking in tongues and she said that maybe he was. Maybe the Lord was trying to reach down into his soul through the dream.

The buzz of the water in the tub/Jacuzzi was the only sound. Now and then, a water pipe gurgled in the high rise as another resident on another floor used the bathroom above or below him. He was on the fourteenth floor and the lake view cost him $2,500 a month. Hell, that was chickenfeed. Besides, he lived in the city now because he was afraid of driving cars. He was going to have to sell the farm anyway, that was pretty clear. Once Helen made up her mind.

She had been born and raised in Chicago. She said she'd never leave the city. Well, he could put up with that. He didn't think much one way or the other about Chicago. He had laid a lot of Chicago girls in his time and he still liked to go out eating now that he couldn't drink anymore, and the city was good for that. But that was about as much as he ever thought about it. He just didn't want to be driving again. Never again. He had been behind the wheel a few times but each time, it was a bad experience. He'd end up with nightmares from driving. So selling the farm was a good idea from that point of view too, because driving was about the only way to get around Caswell.

It wasn't that Helen wouldn't be safe in Caswell. But he could see it from her point of view. He was beginning to see things from a lot of points of view. He was amazed he could change as much as he'd changed. He could even see things from Eddie Briggs's point of view, but the general manager was still a pissant cocksucker. No use getting carried away.

He lifted himself out of the tub using the bar imbedded in the tile wall for leverage. His body dripped water on the fluffy bathroom rug but his legs felt good. Not good exactly but better. He couldn't remember before the accident when his legs had never felt anything at all.

Helen had got him ten night pills. The night pills didn't interfere with his swing or vision or coordination. They were mild and eased the pain so that he could sleep. They weren't sleeping pills because Helen didn't believe in that. It was so wonderful to discover each day the things that Helen thought about the things he had always taken for granted.

At the beginning of the thing, he took pain shots in the locker room just like football players. But the numbness affected his play in the field. He had always been a slow sort of outfielder with bursts of brilliance, and the Novocain slowed him to sloppiness. Manager Riley even benched him for a couple of games and he couldn't stand that. He had stopped using the shots most of the time.

Helen said that because he walked now with pain, he appreciated walking all the more. And it was true. They walked on the lakefront through Lincoln Park so that he could strengthen his legs and he felt triumphant to be able to do such a thing. Helen made him feel proud of himself and he hadn't felt that off the field in a long time.

Like Millie up in Montana, going to school, what was this, the sixth year? Four years of boarding school, two of college, God knew how many more before she decided she'd had enough. Christ, it seemed to take kids a long time these days to get through school. Girl was damn near twenty, should be out rustling up a boyfriend. And how was he going to ever explain Helen to Millie?

Well, maybe Millie would understand.

It was plain that Mae didn't. Not from the git-go. Not as though he and Mae were ever going to get back together again—what was it to Mae what he wanted to do with the rest of his life? All Mae thought about was what Homer owed her for making her his wife when they were both young enough to be in diapers instead of each other's pants.

Hell, Mae was the one let herself get knocked up and he did the right thing, didn't he? It might not even been his kid. Mae didn't come from no convent. Her family was trash.

The thoughts boiled up in him now and he was mad at Mae. What would Helen have said to him now? That he was in no position to ever be mad at anyone, given how he had lived his life so far? Told him that one day when they were walking on the breakfront along Lake Michigan. He got so damned mad at her and called her names and all and she had walked away from him. Just left him, standing there cursing on the lakefront. Damn, he felt low then. She wouldn't talk to him for a week and then only after he had cried an apology to her that had come from his heart. His black heart.

He slipped into bed. The cool sheets felt good to him. He stretched his legs out and the pain was less and less. He wished Helen were sleeping next to him now. He wished he could cuddle her and kiss her and tell her things, tell her stories about his life and being a boy down home and all the things stored up in himself that he had never shared with another person. Not Mae, not Millie. He wanted Helen to look at him with her beautiful hazel-brown eyes and smile at him and tell him that she was proud of him, that he was a good man.

Yes.

He began to fall asleep thinking about it.

He wanted her to tell him he was a good man.

FOURTEEN

MAX HEUBNER was out of pocket. It was an old newspaper term and it meant that he could not be reached. Not called, not seen, not anything if the seeker was named Jimmy Drover.

Drover tried all morning. He even impersonated officialdom. This time he showed up in Heubner's office as a field investigator for the Major Leagues' commissioner's office, but the charmed secretary said that Mr. Heubner was not in town and no, she didn't know when he would return and, no, she didn't know where he was.

"Helluva way to run a business," is what Drover said.

So he and Lori spent the day and evening in the rainy city looking for rainbows and finding them everywhere. They rode a ferry in Puget Sound and they listened to the foghorns and buoy bells at night from a small French restaurant in the market.

Seattle is really a roughneck city despite the cooing image of the Frugal Gourmet and precious little coffee houses. Men with flannel shirts and black beards swing through the streets of the town and there are gambling dens behind many a saloon wall. Drover and Lori Gibbons fed themselves on the charms of the city until midnight, when they went to a room in the Olympia Hotel and made love to each other.

When they were finished with the first act, they made love in the second act by cuddling and talking to each other.

"If I settled down, would you marry me?" he said.

"I don't want to settle down."

"One plane looks much like another."

"I haven't finished traveling. I don't know if I ever will. And you'd want children."

"Only if I grow up."

"There's that problem too," she said.

Around dawn, they made love again. This time it was very long and physical and it was full of kisses and moans. When they kissed, they made funny sounds that would have amused them if they heard a soundtrack of it.

It amused the men who had bugged the room.

There were two of them and they listened and hooted. One of them said, "Go for it, Drover, drill her." The other said, "Oh, honey, I love you so much." They were very amused and thought they were amusing.

The bugs were all connected to a transmitter that was stuck on a window in the room. The transmitter, in turn, used a very low frequency to send the sounds of the room to a van parked on the street below where a receiver fed the sounds into a tape machine. And the two men, amused by the sounds of lovemaking, were in the van.

They ordered breakfast from room service and took turns in the shower. They were both dressed when room service wheeled the cart into the room. The eggs were fresh and so was the fruit. Drover signed and tipped in cash. He always tipped in cash even though he knew the IRS was making it harder for waiters and waitresses to be able to steal for a living. It was the principle of the thing.

He started calling at eight.

Heubner answered the phone this time in a sleepy voice. He hadn't expected persistence.

"I don't know you, I don't know what you want."

"That's bullshit, Max. I know you. And now you've sent over your girlfriend to involve me in some cockamamy plot or scenario or whatever you've got going. We've got to meet and talk about things."

"I can't be seen. You work for a Vegas oddsmaker."

"I promise, he donates to Catholic Charities and is kind to his mother. If that doesn't do it, I want to talk to you about Leonardo and the other guy you sent around to rattle my cage. I want to know what the fuck it is that you want."

"Mae said you wouldn't talk to her."

"Talk to her? She's just a scenario. I want to talk to the screenwriter himself."

"I can't talk to you. There are rules in baseball. Besides, my partners would not—"

"Max, you are not my favorite person on earth but I still want to see you and we're just going to keep doing this until you see me."

"What did I do to you? Where do I know you from?" Said in a tough-guy way, without moving the lips very much.

"I'll tell you when I see you."

"All right." Pause. A weariness crept into the voice. "You should have seen Mae. You should have listened to her."

"I listened but she wasn't saying anything."

"Maybe I got nothing to say."

"Maybe so. Maybe it's me and it's not Mae."

"I don' want you to come round my office no more like you did yesterday. You go down to the Space Needle, in the park, I'll meet you there around nine thirty."

"OK. But don't be real late."

"Do I know what you look like?"

"Don't worry. I know what you look like, Max."

Down in the van, the tapes shut down.

The first man said, "What do you think he wants to tell him?"

The second man said, "We can nail that asshole later. We better call Frank and get a scope in the park so we can listen in."

"Don't we need another court order for that?"

"That beats the shit out of me. Leave it to the lawyers in the office. I was an accountant, not a lawyer. So here I am, sitting in a van in the middle of Seattle. You never know how things are going to turn out."

"I was just thinking we might need another court order. Frank wouldn't want this fucked up—he's been on this one for too long."

"The one'll fuck it up is the district attorney, not us. Once they get in the courtroom, they cut their deals just like all lawyers. Order, schmorder. Just do your job."

"I'd like to hear them fucking again. God, it was hilarious."

"Yeah." That made the ex-accountant smile. "Yeah, you remember how they went?" Then he made a sound imitating an orgasm and they both laughed about it.

FIFTEEN

HOMER ADMINISTERED the needle to his knees. First one, then the other. The Novocain dripped in and he could feel the tingling numbness gradually spread over the knees as he finished dressing. He didn't have a game today.

The doorman called on the phone at 10:00 A.M. and announced Helen. He went to the door and opened it and waited for her. The elevator door opened and there she was. She smiled at him and came to him. His knees hardly hurt at all. They were hardly there. He wouldn't mention the Novocain to Helen because he didn't want her to know that he had his own supply now and he shot himself every day when he wasn't playing. Sometimes three times a day. He felt guilty about it.

She was wearing a light brown sweater and brown slacks and walking shoes. She had a wide smile full of perfect teeth. But it was her hazel-brown eyes. He had loved those hazel-brown eyes from the beginning, even when she was lashing him through the bar exercises, making him take that next step and the next, putting him on the weight machine, making the atrophied leg muscles come back when all they wanted to do was sleep. Those lovely eyes that could command him to do anything.

He kissed her for a long moment. When she responded, it prolonged the kiss. When their faces parted, their bodies held together.

"I missed you," he said.

"I missed you. You looked terrific last night in Denver. Why'd you go out in the fifth inning?"

"Oh, they didn't need me."

"It was the knees."

"It was kind of cool. Humid. It was hurting a little."

"You use the needle?"

"No, I didn't have to. I was pretty good, wasn't I?"

"You're the best, Homeboy." She called him homeboy because it had needled him from the beginning, her calling him by that black term. Now it was their joke, another shared intimacy. He was her Homeboy, all right.

They took a long, long walk on the lakefront. They started at Oak Street Beach by the Drake Hotel and walked all the way north to Belmont Harbor. There are beaches along the shore and there is a park that separates the waters of the lake from the wall of high-rise apartments along Lake Shore Drive. It was cool and bright and there were runners sharing the path and bicyclists and old men walking old dogs.

He had never much cared for cities until he met her. Still didn't much care for them. A ballplayer spends his life on the road and cities blur in mind. A city is a hotel and maybe a meal and maybe a bus trip to the airport. Cities have drunks sitting around in the twenty-dollar seats throwing shit on the field, calling you names, telling you what an asshole you are. Cities have groupies waiting around the players' gate after the games, wanting you to squeeze their tits and sign your name on their bellies. Cities. They were all the same, all in a night's work. But Helen was changing that in him too. He was feeling more at home in Chicago, where he had played ball all these years. He saw a little of what she saw here. She knew so damned much about Chicago that you couldn't help but learn something about it.

"I'm puttin' the farm up for sale, called ole Buddy Gooch this mornin'," he said. He had been waiting to tell her all during the road trip what he was going to do. It was his surprise, like springing a diamond on her. Helen wouldn't have taken a diamond.

They were walking apart but now he took her arm and their pace slowed. A freighter steamed almost at the horizon line far out in the lake. She looked straight ahead.

"Why'd you decide that?" she said.

"I decided I ain't goin' back to Caswell. Except to visit now and then. I don't wanna drive no car no more, for one thing. And Caswell ain't got the lure for me no more. You know that, Helen." He wished he had a nickname to offer her but he was too shy about such things and, besides, he loved her name.

"Maybe you'll change your mind at the end of the season," she said in her soft, sure voice. She laid things out in a direct way all the time, never pushing down too hard on the words and never letting up on them either. It was the patient voice of the professional therapist who must cut through self-pity and real suffering and reach for the heart and soul of the victim and raise them up, dragging a crippled body with his rising heart.

"I been thinking about it a long time and it's a good time to put it on the market. Get top dollar for it, too. Three hundred acres and the Japs building that auto plant right in town—goddamn, Caswell ain't seen such prosperity since a load of pigs fell off a trailer truck."

She laughed. Sudden, sharp, bright.

His one gift for her was this ability to make her laugh. He knew she thought he was a corny redneck just fell off a turnip truck and, by God, he was, but he was amusing in his own way. He smiled to make her laugh.

"Homeboy," she said, this time taking her turn in taking his arm. The trees in the park were greening in that slow, northern spring way and the grass was slower still. But it was spring. There were birds and the smell of the earth and lake.

"Homeboy, where are you going then?"

"Goin' up to Chicago, make mah fortune," he said in an exaggerated black southern accent. "Hear' the money just fallin' off the trees up in Chicago."

"You got no skills, Homeboy, whatcha gonna do, open a hot dog stand?"

"Could be. Ahm a fair country cook if I do say so. All them celebrities get their own restaurants, I might do it myself. Specialize in genuine Ozark recipes."

"Ugh," Helen said.

"Honey, you never ate better than Southern and you know it. Fried green tomatoes and chicken-fried steak, yams and—"

"Stop. It's too much this early in the morning," she said.

"—then grits and cracklin' and—"

She punched him on the shoulder and he stopped and they laughed a little more together. One good laugh led to one good kiss and a good holding on to each other that was witnessed by the world in Lincoln Park.

"I love you, honey," Homer said.

"Homeboy, I love you, but we got to think about this thing. Really think about it."

"Nothin' to think about. You got your work and your work is here, I understand that. I understand your feelin' about going down to Caswell and I accept that. You're right."

"It's not a matter of right. That's what you don't understand at all."

By the look on his face, he certainly didn't.

"It's a matter of separate things," she said. "Poor Homer." She touched his cheek. "You think you want to give up everything for me just as a gift, you think that three or four or five years down the line you won't regret it."

"Honey, we can live in Chicago. I lived here half a year for damned near eighteen years as it is. Cubs would take care of me if I wanted to play out here—"

"Why don't you, Homer? Why don't you stop hurting yourself to prove . . . what do you want to prove?"

"I prove it, Helen, I'm showing the sons of bitches. Showed them

Rockies the other night, popped two right over the wall on them, showed them what the old man could do. Helen, if I was at the end of my career, I'd be content. They wanted to bury me and I thought it was right, I'd just jump in the box myself and pull the lid on it. But Eddie Briggs, the dirty son of a bitch, thinks I'm gonna have to kiss the Cubbies' ass—"

"Why is it always Eddie Briggs?"

He had never told her. Never really told anyone. They were on a breakfront formed by huge, square boulders lined up as a seawall of three levels. He went to one of the rocks. "Siddown, Helen."

They sat, hand in hand, on the seawall, staring at each other. The waves lapped meekly at the rocks; the lake waters began to run whitecaps farther out. The wind was picking up suddenly, the way it does in spring.

"Eddie was manager of the Milwaukee Brewers in nineteen eighty-two, eighty-three, right in there." He paused and looked at her in an anxious way. "I'm testifying now, honey, I'm telling you the truth of things because I love you. You know what a rotten sinning son of a bitch I been in my life with drinking and gambling and whoring and I want you to know, that's all past now."

Helen Brown didn't say anything. She stared at him with those awful hazel eyes that could burn a hole in Homer's soul, even in the days when he thought he didn't have any.

He cleared his throat. "Well, honey, Eddie was just a guy who couldn't stop poaching. I saw him a couple of times in Milwaukee and he had different girls when I happened to know he had one of the cutest little honeylambs back home that I ever laid eyes on. And Milwaukee is not that big a town, you know, you start carrying on and what goes around, et cetera. So I know she has to know—Lu Ann."

He paused then. He might be thinking of the image behind the name.

He said the name again.

Helen noticed that.

He cleared his throat.

"From Little Rock, it turns out. One night in the off season, I was up in Little Rock doing a little tomcatting and I run across them, both of them, they were building a place down there even though he was a Georgia boy, but he didn't have no kin left alive.

"Well, honey, he and Lu Ann didn't have no kids, I want you to know that. Well, I was with this sweet thing, no use in mentioning her name if I could remember it, but we did couples that night, dining and drinking and dancing, the whole thing and I see that Eddie Briggs got big eyes for my sweet thing and Lu Ann, she sees it too, and one bottle of booze leads to another and then there's this quiet look in her eye and she says to Eddie that she's tired and she's going home and she's gonna let the three of us party on alone. And she says she's takin' the car and he says she's too drunk to drive and then I find myself saying I'll take her home. I don't know why I said that."

He shook his head and then looked down at the rocks. Someone had graffitied a sentiment at his feet. A.H. loves Lisa.

"Now, it was Eddie's place not to let me take her home. I think that to this day. But Eddie, he's already been sliding his hands all over my girl's fanny on the dance floor, dancing close and shoving his cock against her lap like that, and I know his eyes are bigger than a nigra kid looking in a white toy shop—"

He stopped himself.

Shook his head.

"I'm sorry, honey." She absolutely hated that kind of talk and mostly he never said things like that, but sometimes, even now, he just put his foot in shit and wiggled it around.

She took her hand away from his. And waited.

"Took her home myself. And she told me to come in and I knew what was going to happen. And it did. She was doing it against Eddie and it wasn't me, it might of been someone else. I mean, it just happened."

"That one time."

There was no tone in her voice.

It was terrible and Homer felt how terrible it was. But he was going through with it. He shook his head.

"No, honey. Not that one time."

"You kept on."

"We kept on an Arkansas winter. She'd go out shopping or something and I was sneaking around, renting hotel rooms in the suburbs, you know."

"And he found out."

" 'Course. That was the point of it. I mean, from Lu Ann's point of view. I see that now. I don't know what I was thinking then except I was thinkin' 'bout Lu Ann. I was a single man and Eddie knew something was going on, Lu Ann was shopping or something every chance she got and she was making it easy for Eddie to know something was going on. He was a fairly dumb son of a bitch and still is, but he wasn't that dumb and when he laid it on her, slapped her around a little, she told him. Then he was gonna get a shotgun and come down to Caswell and blow that motherfucking Homer White to hell but, hell, that wasn't gonna happen. Chickenshit son of a bitch."

"So what happened?"

"Nothing. They stayed married. Still are married. I saw her once last season at Wrigley Field. She was coming out of his office and I was going in and I bet Eddie arranged it that way. She's older, hell, we're all older. I said 'hello' or something and I went into his office then. And sat myself down on his leather couch and he just sat there for a long time behind his big old desk, looking at me. Then he said I was playing pretty horseshit for what I was making and I had to agree that was true. I was trying then not to tell anyone about my knees, about the hurting, I was taking the needle on the QT. But he must of known. He just sat there, talking about how horseshit I was and I got hot then the way I used to do and I said if he didn't like it, he should trade me. Trade me into the American League, I could do a DH for someone. That's when I began thinking about fuck the Cubs, I'm gonna finish this thing out because I knew, I *knew* I could still hit a country lick."

"And?"

He looked up and out across the lake. It is as wide as the ocean. The freighter on the horizon was gone and the lake was empty, swollen with whitecaps. The wind was very chill now and the bright, sunny day was clouding up.

"He ain't gonna trade me. He wants me to grind it down. He told the president of the team that they needed me in left field, that he had to keep using me, and that maybe I just had a bad year. But I did have a bad year last year and then I heard from Mae. Mae said that this small five percent partner in the Mariners would take me on the team but that Eddie Briggs said he wanted a draft choice and two long relievers from Seattle and the price was too high because my contract is too high for a man who is going to be pushing forty at the end of the year. See? He's gonna screw me because I screwed his wife."

"So why play for him?"

"I ain't, honey. I'm playing for myself. For you. You got me my legs back. You made me see what courage is. You lifted me."

Damn, he was so happy. He took her small, strong hand in his. He squeezed her hand. She saw that he was happy, that he was confessing to her because he loved her.

"You did it yourself," Helen said.

"You lifted me. You put my foot on the right path. You made me walk. You made me see myself and I faced up to what I was, a worthless piece of shit ever walked as a man."

"You're not worthless, Homeboy. No one is worthless."

"God, I love you, Helen. I love you, I love you."

"That's a terrible story, Homer."

"It's terrible what I done, what everyone's done. Everyone does bad things, don't they? Except you, honey, you."

"Oh, I don't know what to say to you." Her hands gripped his and her eyes, usually so sure, looked as confused as he had ever seen them.

"Quit it," Helen said. "Baseball. You don't have to work no more for Eddie Briggs. What's done is done. If you did wrong, so did his wife and so did Eddie Briggs. You're not a slave. No one's a slave."

"I can't. I can't let that son of a bitch get me. I'm gonna play and hit and then I'm gonna go to the president myself and tell him I wanna go to the AL, maybe Seattle, and tell him to let me go. They'll get something for me after a year like I'm gonna have and Eddie Briggs won't be able to stand in the way of it."

"Tell him now. The president of the team. About what happened."

"That would be wrong, all wrong. Honey, you are showing me right things and that is definitely something I might have done but I can't do no more. I can't shame Lu Ann and I . . . I just can't. That isn't right. What was wrong is gone and two wrongs don't make a right. You see that."

It was so cold now when it had been bright and sunny. The weather shifts so quickly on spring days. They were miles from home, alone on the rocks along the lake, watching fog creep in to smother the city.

It was so very cold.

SIXTEEN

"How do we know each other?"

Max Heubner was wearing a tan raincoat and was bareheaded. He was walking around Drover under the Space Needle monument. He was squinting at Drover as though he couldn't get the connection.

Drover took his time starting up.

"Heubner Construction had a contract fifteen years ago to build moderate-income housing on the West Side of Chicago. You were part of the consortium, all government funding—it was one of those deals that's so complicated it never gets written about the right way. And then it turned out that the housing was very upscale and you, being the out-of-towner, paid off your partners and packed your bags and went back to Seattle before anyone knew it was all a bad deal. Bad for working-class people looking for housing and bad for the G, and when the mortgages collapsed Uncle had to bail it out on the back end."

Drover said this like a reporter talking to his editor about an old story.

Max Heubner shrugged and smiled. "Good days then. I was building for limited partnerships all over the country. Dentists and doctors and lawyers were tax sheltering in shopping centers, housing, all kinds of things. Then it was all knocked out by that Tax Act in eighty-six. Well, I made out OK. But there was nothing crooked about that Chicago deal."

"Like I said. I knew about it because I was friends with David Priest. He did the story for the *Sun-Times*."

"David Priest. Little cocksucker, he was like a terrier on my heels."

"You had too much money to shove into Republican pockets then to get indicted like you deserved."

"Like you got indicted in L.A.?"

Drover just stared at him then. It was going to rain, it had rained, it might rain—it was just Seattle being Seattle. The park was very green and tropical in its lushness. The Needle itself looked curiously old-fashioned, though it had been the way of the future during the '62 fair.

"What's Priest doing?" Heubner asked, smiling, trying to make up a little but doing it in a tough way. The two men were walking in the park, around the needle, their voices low and their hands in their coat pockets.

"He's a reporter at *The Wall Street Journal*. He's still going after crooks."

"He should of been a cop then."

"What is your deal with Homer White?"

"Good ballplayer. Hit two the other night."

"I saw the game."

"Did you?" A neutral voice.

"You talk to Mae?"

"Mae?"

"Come on, Heubner."

"Mae Tilson. I do business with her from time to time. Use her in the market. I'm into a lot of things."

"Mae among them."

"I fucked her, if that's what you're driving at. I fuck a lot of girls."

"What do you really want Homer for? He's thirty-nine years old, Max. Nobody wants a four-year contract on a thirty-nine-year-old ballplayer. That's why the Cubs fired the last general manager who signed it."

"Mae said you should talk to Eddie Briggs. Find out why he won't let Homer come to Seattle. We could use him as a DH. Shit. I could use a guy fifty years old as DH as long as he still had the eye and could still shake the stick."

"You talk like you're sole owner. I checked on that. Five percent. Vanity money, lets you wear World Series rings in the unlikely event the Mariners ever get into a World Series."

"I take an interest in baseball. I always been interested in sports."

"You're interested in Mae Tilson. But she hasn't been married to Homer for a very long time. You doing Mae a favor? You showing her your clout?"

"I don't have to show her shit."

"She hasn't been married to Homer for a long, long time."

"I know that."

Silent walking. Feet on wet grass. A grumble of thunder. The park was empty at this time of morning.

"Max, why did you sic those Vegas dogs on me? First, you want me to lay some shit on Homer. Fine, I understand why you would use me. Because I might have a grudge and I do have connections in the newspapers. But it's so clumsy. Then you sic Mae on me and want me to investigate Eddie Briggs of the Cubs for no reason."

"You know that Eddie Briggs might have a hard-on for Homer too?"

"Is that right? That's what Mae tried to imply before I so rudely insulted you in front of her and she left the restaurant. Good restaurant, though. I hope she left a decent tip. I hate to have women pick up the bill because, most of the time, they leave a lousy tip."

"I'm sure she did. Mae's been around."

"So what did she want to tell me about Eddie Briggs that I might possibly want to know?"

"Homer used to bang his old lady," Max Heubner said. "He's got a grudge. At least one guy still has the balls to keep hating." He stared at Drover. They had stopped walking.

"So what? Baseball is like any business. You do bottom-line stuff."

"He says he'd trade with us for a number-one draft and two long relievers. We might as well throw in the Kingdome while we're at it."

"Then you don't want Homer bad enough."

"I'm willing to talk our GM into taking a chance on that contract of his. Imagine a thirty-nine-year-old guy with bag legs sitting on six million guaranteed over four years."

"Eddie say he had bad legs? Or was that Mae?"

"It's common knowledge."

"It's common knowledge where, Max?"

"You're in Vegas, you don't even know?"

"Common knowledge where? Does your GM know he has bad legs?"

"He was in an accident, for Christ's sake. He broke his legs. He was lucky to come back."

"So why pick up a cripple? Even for DH? That's taking a chance. What if he can't walk next year?"

Heubner said, "Just say I want him."

"Any which way you can."

"Any which way."

"Shit, Max. You just want him out of Chicago. Either get him investigated out of baseball or get him in Seattle. Either way, get him out of Chicago. I finally connected all the dots, didn't I?"

Max stared at him. Drover thought he was beginning to guess better.

"What is it, Max? What's your grudge with Homer? Everyone has one. He hasn't been leading a blameless life as far as I know. Eddie hates him for having an affair with his wife. Says you. And Mae . . . why does Mae hate him exactly?"

"Mae don't hate him. Mae wants to help him. He told her he was hurting and she comes to me and says that he would love to go into the American League to finish his career as a DH. You see the way he's hitting this spring? Am I right about him or what?"

"You talk like a Mariners fan, all pumped up by three weeks of baseball. It's a very long season, Max. If Homer is hurting now, he's gonna be hurting a lot more in September."

"I'm used to being a gambler. Taking a chance."

"Which brings up Elmore Leonardo and his friend from Vegas."

"I never go to Vegas. They wouldn't have me as a partner if I was consorting with people like you."

"People like me hold their noses when consorting with people like you, Max."

"You don't look tough to me, Drover. I started out in high steel, you know that? Ironworker. I take care of myself, I could take you, you know that? Nobody in the park—I could take care of you."

"Maybe I could take care of you. Go to the commissioner and lay it all out about your two gonzo friends and their crap evidence and Mae Tilson and the deals you work and—"

"And you'd tell him why, right? You'd get so far and then he'd say, 'Why would Mr. Heubner be doing any of this?' and you wouldn't have an answer and the commissioner would tell you to go back to your rathole in Cruz."

"And don't call me in Santa Cruz or have your bimbo call me," Drover said.

He wanted what came next.

Good right hand, diamond ring, hair on the knuckles, and just a little slow.

Drover stepped into him with two fast ones to the upper chest.

Drover didn't expect the left so fast. He was looking for a second right. It caught him on the side of the head, dead on the right ear.

Then he went down on one knee and Heubner did an imitation of a placekicker. The football went right between the uprights. That is to say, Drover caught the shoe right under the collarbone and flew back, arms akimbo. Max Heubner came up then and kicked three times more at his side, breaking ribs and tearing muscle.

Drover just lay there with blood coming from his nostrils and his right ear.

"Asshole," Max Heubner said. He was running out of breath. It was starting to rain. "Asshole," he said again.

After the last two words, the tapes in the van parked by the concession area stopped.

SEVENTEEN

FRANK CHESROW was the assistant United States attorney in charge of the investigation. He had wires all over Seattle. He had Heubner wired and Mae wired and he had wired Drover once Drover came up in conversation. Actually, he forgot how Drover had come up.

This was all out of the fertile brain of Al Pardee.

Frank Chesrow, who wore white shirts and cuff links, probably thought he was better than Al Pardee because of what Al Pardee had been.

Was.

Al Pardee was sitting across from Frank Chesrow now in Chesrow's office in the federal building downtown. The door was closed.

"I wasted enough time on Drover. Whatever this shit is about, I'm not interested," Frank Chesrow said. He looked down at his tie. He looked at Al Pardee's tie. He like his own tie better. Al Pardee was a fat slob. He wore an old-fashioned fedora. He looked like a gangster and he talked like one. He had the morals of a rat.

"I tole you, Frank. Heubner hires Elmore for a side job. He wants to get this Homer White out of Chicago. His ex–old lady wants him in Seattle. She is banging with Heubner. I mean, does she want to get married to him again or what? And why would Max do that kind of favor for her if he was already banging her?"

Frank shook his head then. He held up his hand to stop the words.

"Cut it out, Al. You make me crazy. Who's banging who—who cares? We put a wire on Mae Tilson and it gets us nothing. She makes a call to her ex-husband in Chicago. He tells her he's met a woman and he's coy about it, won't tell her much. So this is soap opera stuff, what the fuck does it have to do with our business? You work for me, Pardee, remember? I don't work for you. Uncle doesn't work for you."

"I just think about Drover. I think about him all the time. I been thinking about him for ten years."

"So what? What's that to me? I don't care about nobody named Drover," Frank Chesrow said. "Unless he's part of our investigation."

"You guys told me it was Drover that tied a can to my tail down in L.A. in nineteen eighty-three on that big conspiracy indictment. He used my name to cut his own deal with you people. Who's the only guy indicted got to walk? Drover. Not even day one of time out of it."

"You people, you people. I don't want to hear that. Whatever went down in L.A. was in the court of the attorney there. It had nothing to do with me. I didn't even know you existed in nineteen eighty-three."

Al Pardee shook his fat head and his jowls jiggled and his piggy eyes were hard. "I hate that geek son of a bitch. I had three years inside to think about that geek son of a bitch. I think about him taking a walk in the fresh air and me, I walk around in a yard the size of a playpen. I think about him for three years and I think every possible thing I can about him. Some geek I barely knew at all sends me up."

"How do you think he managed that?"

"To save his ass," Pardee said. He wasn't listening to Chesrow. He wasn't even following a line of argument. How did the G do any of its miracles? The one prosecutor had taunted him, said that Drover was walking out on the multiple indictments as a free man, and he gave Pardee the needle about it and Pardee had shrugged it off. At first. Then, more and more, he thought about it. He talked to a couple of guys over the years inside the joint. He fashioned his conspiracy theory about the conspiracy indictment that sent a bus full of mobsters to prison. How was it that this one geek walked?

Now he sat in the cool gray office of the U.S. attorney and stared through Chesrow like he didn't exist. The only thing that mattered to Al Pardee was Drover. When he had used Elmore Leonardo on that errand that night in Seattle, he wondered if Drover would remember what he looked like. Prison is supposed to take off weight, but in three years inside, he had gained a hundred pounds and developed breathing problems and all kinds of little ailments. No, Drover hadn't recognized him at all. Not that they had ever been friends.

How could the geek have taken him down? He barely knew the geek. But he couldn't ignore the fact that he did three years inside and that the mocking prosecutor told him it was all compliments of Drover. If he needed any more proof, it was in the fact that Drover never spent a night in prison.

Across the desk, Chesrow watched Pardee. Chesrow watched the fat man form silent words with his fat lips. The fat man was staring and staring, and it amused Chesrow. To an extent.

"Come on back to the real world, Al," Chesrow said.

Al blinked and looked at him.

"Get off this shit with Drover and Mae Tilson and Homer White—this is all side show. You're our snitch inside. Our informant. On the mob and the mob's businessman, Mr. Heubner."

"What's important to me isn't gonna interfere with what you want, Mr. Chesrow," Al Pardee said.

"It interferes because it disables your attention span, limited as it already is."

Al Pardee stared at him.

"I want a big name for myself in Seattle. I don't intend to mess with major league baseball. Or some broken-down ex-sportswriter who lives in Santa Cruz like a bum. Small fish and dangerous waters both."

Al Pardee stared.

"Capeesh?" said the prosecutor, who thought he should throw in a little Italian to show he was tough.

Al nodded, a barely recognizable nod. The nod was short and simple, though Chesrow would not get the message of the nod.

The nod said: Fuck you.

EIGHTEEN

They kept Drover in King County Hospital overnight. They taped his ribs, bandaged his concussion, and applied painkillers. He would live, but he would not be pretty for a few days. He was so groggy from the drugs that he slept the clock around, lost in a fog of dreams that reached back to days of his boyhood.

In the morning, Drover dressed before the breakfast cart came into the unprivate room. The nurse's aide pushing prunes and Special K was displeased. Drover said it was all right, he never ate breakfast anyway.

They left the room together, and thirty minutes later he was free and clear of the hospital. He wanted to call Lori to see if she was still at the Olympia wondering what happened to him. But he had wanted to get out of the hospital more.

He walked across the wet lawn to the street and the car pulled up just as he stood at the stoplight and wondered where he might find a pay phone.

The two men who climbed out were dressed in white shirts and blue ties and wore gray suits. They might have been wearing uniforms.

But they showed him identification anyway. "I guess this means you're not going to take me someplace to beat me up?" Drover smiled at one.

He didn't smile back.

Drover got in the back seat and the second agent placed his hand on the top of Drover's head so he would not crack it again on the way in. The hand made his head hurt. Drover said so.

The drive downtown to the federal building produced no conversation.

Drover tried. "Are these cars good on mileage?"

Silence.

"Did you hear the one about J. Edgar Hoover and the hula skirt?"

"Shut the fuck up," said the man sitting next to him.

"Oh," Drover said.

They left him in a waiting room. He asked to use the phone. He wanted to call Lori at the hotel. His head hurt. His brain was groggy with painkillers, which weren't working all that well. They said he couldn't use the phone.

Ten minutes later, he was escorted into Frank Chesrow's office. The office was decorated with pictures of President Clinton, the new chief of the FBI, the Democratic attorney general, and other saints of the current federal church.

The United States attorney had a clean desk, which meant he was tidy or he had very little to do. Drover commented on this in what he thought was a cheerful way.

"Siddown."

Drover sat.

"What's your connection with Max Heubner?"

"Connection?"

"Cut the crap."

"All right."

Silence.

"I asked you a question," Chesrow said.

"I thought we were cutting the crap."

"I asked you a question, smart guy."

"Oh. I thought that was part of the crap. Why don't you ask Heubner?"

"Don't tell us what to do."

"OK."

Silence.

"You were indicted on conspiracy charges of gambling and racketeering—"

"Ten years ago. It was bullshit. You should know that."

"I don't know that. I know you walked. Sometimes, the little fish swim out of the net."

"Did Izaak Walton say that?"

"You're a gofer for a Vegas oddsmaker named Fox Vernon."

"Am I?"

"I asked you about Max Heubner."

"You were there watching me, weren't you? One of your trained monkeys?"

"I'll ask questions."

"No, let me help," Drover said. "You let Max beat me up. Shame on you. I thought my tax dollars ensured a swift, prompt response from the FBI."

"I'm not with the FBI."

"But you're using them. What's it got to do with Max? You finally moving in on the rat?"

"What do you know about him?"

"Just what I used to read in the newspapers."

"What about his friend? Mae Tilson?"

"Are you investigating her too?"

Chesrow didn't like this. He decided that all of a sudden. He got up and went to the window wall and stared at the foggy city all around them. "Don't get in the middle of something."

"I can't believe you were tailing me and watched me getting beat up by Max Heubner," Drover said. "I'm shocked at the callous lack of response on the part of my FBI. I've a good mind to send my Junior G-Man badge back to Kellogg's."

"You want to be part of this, Drover? You want in, I can arrange to bring you in. Is that what you want?"

"What I want is to be left alone. Ten years ago, your colleagues in L.A. could have left me alone. They indicted me because it made the indictment look pretty. Two dozen Sicilians and one genuine WASP sportswriter. The Sicilians got jail. I got fired from the only job I wanted. Now you can't booga-booga me because I don't work for anyone."

"You work for Fox Vernon."

"You investigating Fox Vernon?"

"Should I?"

"Beats me. He always seemed like a nice enough fellow to me but you never know. Still waters run deep."

"You like to talk nonsense, don't you? I want to know why Max Heubner and you had a tiff."

"Don't they make bugs anymore? You mean you didn't have it all bugged? When did you start bugging me? Yesterday? A week ago? I think I need a lawyer."

"You do something wrong?"

"No, I think you did. Someone from the ACLU. A discreet press conference or two."

"You wanna drag yourself through the mud again?"

"You do it once, you don't have to think twice about doing it again. You guys burned me once and it hurt for a long time. It doesn't hurt anymore. Nerve endings are shot."

"All right. All right." He turned from the window. "You get out of here."

"No. I don't want to go," Drover said. "I get my chops busted and you guys are sitting around watching. You probably bugged my hotel room. You picked up my friend yet? Talked to her?"

Chesrow said nothing and Drover knew what that meant.

"You low-life bastard," Drover said. "That makes two of us for the ACLU. We can subpoena the tapes you made."

"No one made tapes."

"I know that's a lie."

Silence.

They stared at each other. Suddenly, Chesrow did that little federal smile that says, Let's be friends.

"We're interested in a lot of things connected with Max Heubner."

"Then bug Max. I suppose that's self-evident." And Drover

thought about Lori. Thought about making love with her in that hotel room. Thought of the dirty sound it would make on a tape recording. He got up from his chair then and took a swing at the United States attorney.

Two men were through the door before Drover realized he had missed. Pain pills threw him off. He'd have to get his swing back.

This made him think of Homer White a moment before one of the two men put him in a choke hold and dragged him to the straight chair. It didn't make his head feel better, or his ribs.

Frank Chesrow surprised him then.

"Let him go," he told the two of them.

They released him.

"Go on."

"We'll be right outside."

"It's all right. Go on."

They closed the door behind them.

"Drover."

"No."

"Drover," Chesrow began again.

"The U.S. attorney in Seattle has revealed he is investigating a part owner of the Seattle Mariners baseball team and a star hitter for the Chicago Cubs involved in a federal conspiracy with a previously indicted former Los Angeles sportswriter," Drover said.

"Fuck you. You want to obstruct justice?"

"It's done all the time. I told you: I want to be left alone."

"You're left alone from now. From right now."

"I bet you tell everyone that."

"Damnit. I wanted to talk to you about Heubner."

"And this is about baseball, isn't it?"

"No."

"No?"

"Why on earth would you think I want to get involved in that can of worms? I live in Seattle. I've lived here all my life. We have a team here, one that we've worked very hard to keep. Why would you think I want to involve myself in anything like that?"

Drover stared at Chesrow.

"I bet you have ambitions. Become a senator or something."

Chesrow just managed to conceal most of the blush.

"And our beloved president. A Razorback. Just like Homer White."

The blush filled out a little more.

Drover managed a thin smile. "So this is really just about something else."

"You don't want to know. Or interfere," Chesrow said.

"OK."

Got up with a wince. Stared at Chesrow.

"Just don't interfere with me anymore. Not one more time. Not once more, Chesrow."

No words then.

But they knew what the bargain was. And what it would be.

NINETEEN

Millie called up her mother on Friday to tell her the news.

Millie said Daddy had called her and talked to her for a long time and told her that he loved her and that he was going to sell the farm and he was hoping, if things worked right, that he would be getting married again and what did it mean, Mommy?

It meant Daddy had found someone to live with him and he was selling the farm. He said he was selling the farm? Who was he selling it to?

Millie said Daddy said he was just putting it up for sale because he was going to live in Chicago with this woman he had met. Well, he said he thought she would eventually see it his way. Millie thought Daddy sounded real serious.

So did Mommy.

And later that night, she thought she'd have to do it herself. She was a strong woman and she could do for herself. Max wouldn't put the hit on a ballplayer in Chicago because he wanted to do it the complicated way and because he told her there were rules about killing someone in Chicago and blah blah blah. He said all the things men say when they want to get out of something. He didn't want to get involved in too many people knowing too many things about what he wanted to do.

Besides, Max had his own deals. The farm belonged to her, damnit. It was her inheritance from that son of a bitch who walked out on her, leaving her with the baby and just enough alimony to make living hurt. Homer had had all the glory years without her.

Well, he wasn't going to get away with it. Not anymore.

TWENTY

Lori GIBBONS got to the hospital just after Drover checked out.

She got to the federal building just after he left it.

They met back at the hotel at noon. He was waiting for her because she had left her bag in the room. When she saw him, she went pale.

"Oh, Jimmy," she said.

"It's not that bad. I've been beaten up by better guys," Drover said. He got up from the bed because she wanted a hug. Lori didn't see him wince or hear the *oww* of air that involuntarily escaped him. But she did feel the bandages beneath his shirt.

"Oh." She stepped back. "I didn't mean to hurt you."

"The course of true love is fraught with pain."

"Are you all right?"

"A couple of ribs. It's all right, Lori."

"What happened?"

"I picked a fight with the wrong guy. Second time in the past few days I've done that. Maybe I should learn to be a pacifist while I can still chew hard candy."

"What do you want to do?"

"They talked to you? The FBI guys?"

"Yes. What's this all about?"

"I wish I knew. I'm sorry I got you involved."

"I'm not involved in anything I can't handle."

"Maybe I am."

They took the limousine from SFX to Kelly's place on the pier in Santa Cruz. It's not a cheap way to travel, but Drover leaned hard on his expense account from Fox Vernon to show that newspapermen knew how to do it best. By the time they were in Santa Cruz, Lori had her composure back and Drover felt terrible. The pain pills were working only sporadically. He thought he'd like to have a couple of Red Labels on the rocks to help them along.

Kelly let his jaw drop when he saw Drover's bandaged head. It was a look of pure empathy. Drover used to say, "You can choose your relatives but you can't choose your friends." It was true. Drover got it backwards on purpose because he believed it. Kelly was a friend because he wanted it bad enough to work for it. Not that they both hadn't seen people who looked a lot worse.

"What's up, pal?" Kelly finally said.

"I ran into a guy in Seattle," Drover said. "Lori could use a drink. And I hate to see a lady drink alone."

Kelly himself went behind the bar and took down a bottle of Johnny Walker Red. "I can give you the Black," he said.

"Naw. It'd be wasted on me. I only want it for medicinal purposes anyway."

Nancy, Kelly, Lori, and Drover, sitting around the round table in the back with drinks. Drover said he never wanted to eat again.

"Corned beef brisket, boiled cabbage, and new potatoes," Kelly said in answer.

"A small plate," Drover said.

"A child's portion," Kelly said and went back to the kitchen. He prepared it himself.

Drover began to tell Nancy what had happened. Lori had heard it all on the plane. When Kelly brought out the plates of food, Drover stopped his story to eat. For a man who would never eat again, he did fairly well. They ate the steaming corned beef and dipped the cabbage in horseradish sauce. When Toby came around the bar and cleared the dishes, Drover resumed his narration. He ended it with the conversation in the U.S. attorney's office. He didn't mention that his hotel room had been bugged by the G because it would have embarrassed Lori. Apparently Chesrow had been enough of a gentleman not to mention it to Lori when he questioned her.

"So, what do you think?"

Kelly shrugged. "I think you shouldn't get into any more fights with this Heubner guy. Whatever he's at the center of, you don't need that kind of grief."

Drover smiled. "Now you tell me."

He looked at Nancy.

Nancy Harrington stared right through him the whole time. Her eyes had a faraway look.

He noticed it. He stopped talking but she didn't stop staring through him.

She shrugged then. "We should have a drink," she said.

So it was time for another glass of Scotch. Kelly poured himself a child's portion of VO and water. When the drinks were settled, Nancy suddenly leaned forward, arms on the table, and looked right down deep into Drover.

"What are you going to do?"

He shrugged and paid for it with a grimace.

"This isn't about sports," he said. "This is a domestic matter. Every motive in this thing is a private one. And now I know the G is cooking up something for the bad guy, for this Heubner. So what should I do?"

"What about Homer White?"

"I'm sorry his legs are hurting. But he still makes millions, which is more than I make. And if he's found love and joy with some new someone in Chicago, whoever it is, God bless him."

"Aren't you curious even?" Nancy said.

"I'm paid to get curious about sports."

"Come on, Jimmy."

He stared at her and put down his drink. He shook his head. "I went to Denver and talked to Homer. Nothing to talk about. Homer is having the makings of a good year. Maybe it's love. Maybe he's found Jesus. Homer took a shot at me for my troubles but I persevered. I even got walloped by his ex-wife, Mae. I always thought being the designated hitter meant I got to shake the stick, not that everyone could come and hit me. I don't like to play It when I'm It."

"Why does Mae want to bring him to Seattle?"

"I don't know. Maybe she's missing him, maybe they're just good friends and she wants to help out her current boyfriend, Heubner. I don't know. Motives are complicated in sports like in life, as Ditka might put it. There was a GM once who traded away a twenty-game winner because he didn't like the guy's attitude. Not only traded him but traded him to Texas with the idea that the twenty-game winner would wilt under the heat and humidity of those Arlington, Texas, nights. I know another case, true story, where this GM traded a .330 hitter to San Francisco for a washed-up home-run slugger with the idea that the guy's average would be killed playing night ball in the wind tunnel known as Candlestick Park. Baseball is full of stories like that. Stupid, self-defeating, senseless trades made by people in positions of arrogance."

"But Homer has bad legs," Nancy said. "Being a DH in the American League would let him do what he does best, hit, and let him rest his legs. Nothing you've said makes this something that Mae would want to do for her ex-husband."

"I told you, maybe she's doing it for her new squeeze, Heubner."

"And that's why Heubner sics two goons from Vegas on you," Nancy said. "Makes sense."

"It doesn't make sense. I just don't want to be involved anymore. It makes my ribs hurt."

"You get involved," Nancy said. She was thinking of the time Drover had ridden a white horse to her rescue when a cheapjack gambler from Vegas had made her life misery. Drover had arranged a fixed poker game for the gambler and nearly got killed for his troubles. Nancy knew Drover had been in love with her once, but love is just an easy way to explain doing irrational things, like rescuing a fair damsel.

"That was a long time ago," he said to her, completing the unspoken thought.

"You don't understand," she said.

"Understand what? What is the damned thing I don't understand?"

"No, nothing." She sipped her drink, shook her head. "Like you said, it doesn't involve you."

"Come on, Nancy. Understand what?"

"The woman."

He waited. She said nothing.

"What woman, Nancy? There's more than one. There's the unnamed woman in Chicago that Homer is dating. And the wife of his general manager in Chicago he dated once. Maybe there're too many women."

"Sure. There's only one, Jimmy. Mae Tilson."

"And she's doing him a favor."

"Sure she is."

Nancy was a tough lady. She'd been around Vegas, singing for her supper and trying to keep her husband straight with the gamblers. But her Johnno was seven kinds of a fool, and when the debts had piled up too high he took the easy way out and killed himself.

"Don't get tough, Nancy," Drover said.

"Yeah. Don't get tough. Mae Tilson sounds wonderful. The milk of human kindness flows in her veins. Sounds lovely. She lies to you, she'll even make up to you for the sake of some man she hasn't lived with for nearly twenty years."

Drover put down his drink. "Careful, Nancy." They all knew why. She was circling in on her own black past with dead Johnno.

She shook her head and looked from Kelly to Lori and back to Drover.

"I loved Johnno. Still do. But less every day. Fond memory. Not so fond. He did everything wrong, but he was there. And I was there with him right up until he decided to take the last step alone."

She had tears in her eyes. She wiped them away hard. She took another sip. She slapped the drink down on the table hard. Kelly moved toward her instinctively and grasped her pretty little hand.

"No, Kelly," she said. "You don't see, and neither do you, Drover."

Lori Gibbons said it then: "Mae. Mae is the center."

And Nancy gave her a hard smile. "That's what it's all about, boys."

Lori stared at Nancy, and Nancy's smile was the smile of experience. Perhaps it was even a little cruel. Maybe it was the bitterness of the past mingling with the now. The bad past should stay dead and buried.

But Drover saw it in Nancy's smile too.

She had gotten to the root of the thing.

TWENTY-ONE

Helen brown got off work at 4:00 p.m., threw on her raincoat, and carried her umbrella and big purse out to the street. It wasn't raining but it was cold, the wind keening down the towers on both sides of Michigan Avenue. She waited for the bus on the corner of Ontario. When it came, she climbed in and showed her pass card and moved to the back. It was crowded.

She stood in the aisle, grasping one of the steel bars that have replaced straps in all buses. She was in that sort of commuter state of mind that half reviews the events of the past day and anticipates the evening. The Cubs had played all afternoon and lost to the Brewers at Wrigley Field. It would be hurting him more tonight, she thought, because he hadn't gotten a hit and had been struck out three times.

Losing the eye for the pitch, he called it.

Her father had loved baseball and gone to the games at old Comiskey Park on the South Side. He was a White Sox fan. He had also watched some of the old Negro League games that had been played in the same park for a time before the Jackie Robinson story began to give baseball a different color.

She grew up not loving baseball so much but loving her father. She grew up when baseball was a game heard on radios by men like her father, who would take an afternoon snooze on the back porch of a three-flat and contemplate the world, half asleep and half involved in the game.

She never went to the South Side unless it was to see her mother, who refused to move from that part of the city. It was not her South Side anymore. Not since her father died.

Why was she thinking about it then?

She examined her reverie while standing in the aisle of the bus and thought it must have been because she had thought about Homer striking out and then thought about her father and wondered if her father would have liked to meet someone like Homer White.

They could have sat around the kitchen table and drunk beer from quart bottles like her father always did and talked about baseball. They would have remembered games and plays and old players no longer around. Her father had seen Ted Williams in his day and watched Minnie Minoso play and Nellie Fox and even Joe DiMaggio. Joltin' Joe, he had called him, and smiled at her for the little girl she was in this daydream, sitting at the kitchen table. Joltin' Joe.

The bus swung into the local lanes up Lake Shore Drive.

She made a good living and lived in an apartment condominium in Carl Sandburg Village near North Avenue. It was a section loosely called Old Town and it was honky-tonky on the strip with gilt at the edges. It was a fine neighborhood and she had discovered it when she had struck out on her own nearly fifteen years ago.

What would her mother say of someone like Homer?

She smiled.

On a bus of crowded strangers, her smile was a secret smile. Like all women on public transport, she had learned never to look into another's face for fear of making it seem an invitation. All the strangers on the bus looked away from each other. Some buried themselves in newspapers and a few in books and some just stared into that middle distance that is nothingness.

She got out of the bus at North Avenue. She would end up walking through the park in a long cutback to her apartment building but that suited her. She liked the walk because this neighborhood belonged to her.

She crossed Clark Street.

It was the rush hour and she crossed the wide street like a typical city person, dodging across the lanes, judging the slow cars and the fast ones, the reckless cabs from. . . .

She was nearly run down by a CTA bus.

She just made it to the curb, shaken, on the other side of the street. She stood there a moment, trembling.

"Are you all right, miss?" It was a man in a cap and a white beard. She nodded at him. He said something in sympathy with her about the nature of the CTA and of the bus drivers who used the buses as weapons and then he walked away.

She was just shaken and a stranger had intruded to see if she was all right. Just a stranger.

She had tried to make Homer see it, why she felt so safe and nurtured in the environment of a big city. She saw he tried to see it as well, but there was a lostness in his looking for it. It didn't come naturally to him.

Nice city.

She had told Homer that when she started him walking and he said he had no use for the city, always had lived in the suburbs because the city was full of danger and people of color who hated you just to look at you.

"Are you afraid?" she had asked him once in a soft and teasing voice.

"Yeah, I get scared of things," he had admitted to her then.

She smiled a little bitterly. She remembered his saying it, remembered the tone of his voice.

When she got home, she took a shower and changed her clothes. This was a night for the soft white crepe dress. She would wear the red sash around her waist. She would wear golden earrings on her ears.

Homer White met her at Carlucci's on Halsted Street and they ate an overpriced pasta dinner and drank wine and shared the evening with each other. He was down about the day, about striking out three times.

She asked him if he was in pain.

"To tell you the truth, I took the needle before the game and I don't know, it must change my stride, I can't plant myself right. I ain't gonna take the needle tomorrow. They got Robinson going for them tomorrow—I own that turkey."

"You're getting better, Homeboy. Six months ago you would have said you owned that nigra."

"Honey, I'm just a dumb redneck hillbilly and that's all I been all my life and now I'm learning and I slip, but I keep to the path."

She was smiling.

He smiled back for her, though those three strikeouts hurt more than his legs did now. "Lord loves a sinner who repents."

"Is that what you're doing?"

"Called my daughter the other night like you want me to do. Talked to her so long I gotta buy stock in AT and T. I told her I loved her and that I had that trust fund for her. And I told her I was selling the farm. Got it listed with ole Junior now, best farm agent in the county. I am moving, Helen, I am getting on with my life for a change. Ain'tcha proud?"

He said the last to mask the middle part of his monologue. He was smiling like a salesman and she knew it. She shook her head.

"Homeboy," she said. "I don't want this to go so fast."

"Helen, you're the honestest person I ever knew in the world. When I told you why Eddie Briggs hates me, I felt I lifted it off myself, like before I was lying to you in a way about why I was still on the Cubs and why I was still trying to get someplace by myself. I ain't gonna be dependent on no asshole like Eddie Briggs, no matter what wrong I done him once. The past is the past and we got the future, Helen. I wanna show you I got some integrity to go along with all the bad things. I haven't got round to talking to Mae yet but I will. I mean, about the farm. About sellin' the farm. I'll even take care of Mae somewhat. I just want to cut it off with Caswell, Arkansas, because that ain't no place for a sophisticated woman such as yourself."

"If I'm so sophisticated, what am I doing with a redneck cracker who says ain't?"

"Because you see the pure love I have for you and you take pity on it," he said. It was sincere yet mocking.

Damn.

She suddenly looked away from his shining, smiling face.

Damn, that was close, she thought.

And he saw it.

The smile began to fade.

Damn, damn, he thought.

They looked at each other without words.

The night glittered around them, noisy, full of laughter, drinks, food, people enjoying themselves.

TWENTY-TWO

Dᴿᴼⱽᴱᴿ ᴼᴺᴸʏ packed underwear, socks, a change of sports shirt, and a razor. And a brown envelope that had been sitting in his closet in the apartment at Santa Cruz.

Lori was on her way to San Francisco to take the red-eye for Chicago. Her furlough was up. Maybe that's why Drover decided suddenly not to let the matter rest. Maybe he would have been content to procrastinate on the beach if Lori had been sharing the experience.

Whatever it was, he was back in the city from hell by nine P.M.

The walkway through the terminal at McCarran airport boomed recorded messages from second-rate stars who earn a living in the casinos. Here was the voice of Wayne Newton welcoming you and there was Tony Martin and here was someone who sounded like Tammy Faye Bakker. Are we having fun yet? they all seemed to be saying. Some of the people getting off the plane couldn't wait. They were shoving quarters into the poker machines as fast as they could.

He told the cabbie he wanted the Shamrock and the cabbie knew the way.

*   *   *

At the Shamrock, he paid the cab off and walked through the big casino lobby to the back door that led across the lot to Fox Vernon's oddsmaking headquarters. The sports book itself was in the hotel but this was the place where boys and girls worked their computer magic and Fox Vernon contemplated the mathematics of chance.

Drover waited for Fox for five minutes. The room full of computers hummed with white noise. Here and there, one of Fox Vernon's apparatchiks fooled with figures on a screen in front of him. There is a mathematical base to all gambling, even sports gambling, but it is interrupted by a willful playfulness too. The pro football myth perpetuated by Pete Rozelle when he was commissioner of the game said that on any given Sunday any given team could beat any other given team. Numbers crunchers like Fox Vernon tried to refine that a bit in offering sports lines on games. They did it with statistics and observation of past games. It was even easier to do now with computers to hold the figures.

Drover was never much interested in this aspect of sports. Gambling, for the most part, bored him. He preferred the real thing. Bone on bone, flesh on flesh, will and desire matched against greed and laziness. If he had to admit it, he would say he always rooted for the underdog. Fox Vernon, like all professional gamblers, hoped the underdog would stay under where he belonged.

Fox came out of his office and held the door open. Drover entered and took a seat on a straight chair.

Fox Vernon said, "You look like the Mummy."

"Thank you."

"Who beat you up?"

"Who hasn't?"

"You want to tell me?"

"I want to involve you, you son of a bitch, since you started the ball rolling when you told Elmore I was in Seattle."

"Did he do that?"

"No. But it started everything. I've become the designated hitter. Everyone hits me."

Fox Vernon sat at his desk. He worried the keys of his computer but he wasn't computing anything. It was a form of nervous byplay while Drover began to lay it out for him.

The recitation took ten minutes. He even brought in Nancy's observations on the character of Mae Tilson.

"Nancy Harrington is probably right," Fox Vernon said.

"Women often are," Drover said.

"What I think it might mean is that something bad is going to happen. I don't know who it's going to happen to but I'm betting it's Homer White. Personally, I don't carry water for Homer but nobody deserves—" He let it go, shaking his head.

"Why do you want to get me involved," Fox Vernon said. He said it in a slow way because he knew Drover and he knew Drover was leading up to something.

"Because you got me involved, Fox. You owe me on this. You sent those goons over to me and everything bad that has happened comes from that."

"You think Heubner was using Elmore."

"Yes."

"That wasn't smart of him."

"Elmore himself is a fair imitation of the missing link in the chain of human evolution. When he walks, he scrapes his knuckles on the sidewalk."

"I'm sorry I told Elmore where you were staying," Fox said.

"That doesn't make it right, Foxy. You sent him to Seattle to test me again. To see if down deep in my heart, I was really in the Outfit. I've worked with you off and on for a few years and I didn't deserve that."

"Maybe not," Fox allowed.

"You don't have any close friends, Foxy. I'm as close as it gets. You're getting older and one day, in your senility, you'll look down at the open grave and wonder who's going to mourn for you."

"No, I don't think so. If I'm friendless, perhaps I prefer it that way."

"You are a cold son of a bitch."

"Yes, I am."

Silence. One man waited for the other to break it.

Drover showed him the envelope then. Fox looked at the photograph and at the betting slips recorded on Xerox paper. He said "hmmm" once.

"My gift from Elmore."

"To spread among your former colleagues in the newspaper game."

"I want you to take this back to Elmore and get that monkey off my back. So I can maneuver."

"And do what exactly?"

"Do something about Homer's situation."

"Do you owe him?"

"No."

"Then why do it?"

"Because sometimes you have to do the right thing."

"And me? What do I have to do?"

"You owe me, Foxy."

Fox thought about that. Stroked the keyboard. Thought some more. He looked up without expression. "You want me to talk to the people who can have a heart-to-heart with Elmore. To take him out of the picture."

"There you go," Drover said. "Just make a call."

Fox shook his head. "Not to those cretins. If their phones aren't tapped at this stage, what exactly is the government doing with all our money?"

"You have a point," Drover said.

"I'll make a personal call," Fox said then. He got up. "This settles it."

"This settles what you owe me," Drover said.

"Then I should get going," Fox Vernon said.

He drove his own car to the big hotel and casino at the other end of the Strip. From this point south, the night does not glitter. The desert is vast and silent and frightening in its silence. Vegas has the naturalness of a way station in outer space. Fox pulled into the parking lot, got out of his car and walked into the casino by the entrance near the empty pool. It was cool and he felt alone. The edge of the desert was all around this glittering oasis. Las Vegas makes you think of your mortality, from the parade of aging stars on various stages in town to the circus of Elvis imitators who provide ghostly entertainment. And there is this other thing about the city: It is so phony and bright in its center and then it begins and ends in abrupt darkness in most parts because it was too big in the first place for the environment it was planned for.

This casino, like all the casinos, seemed designed by architects on acid. Against the grandeur of the desert, it was as vulgar as a fart during a Tosca aria. It was just after eleven at night and Drover was sitting back at the Shamrock Casino Hotel, waiting for word from Fox.

Fox was going to have to be the middleman because the man he was going to see was on Fox's level. He just hoped the FBI wasn't currently bugging Sal Marconi as well as tapping his phones.

Marconi was a legitimate oddsmaker with his own following and he was part of the sports-book package in the hotel that was owned 51 percent by certain people who, in turn, were owned 94 percent by other people who were not extremely welcome in the environment of Las Vegas. The gaming commission kept a black book of names and they were in it.

Marconi was a slick man in slick clothes that came from Rodeo Drive. He wore watches and girls to have things on his wrists.

He was all business now but there were a couple of girls anyway, barely contained in outfits you only see in Vegas and in certain porn magazines.

Sal Marconi said, "It's a surprise to see you, Fox."

"It's a surprise for me," Fox Vernon said. He took a leather chair.

"Drink?" One of the girls came running. Or as close to running as you can get on four-inch heels. She was a worker, which meant her waitress costume featured legs and a small amount of satin above. The ornamental women wore a few more inches of clothing.

"Seven-Up," Fox said.

"Get him," Sal said. The woman went away.

"So. Is this a pleasure call or what?"

"One of yours wanted one of mine," Fox began. "So I helped him out with a phone number. This is a week or so ago. I figured it was an errand for you and I was curious what you wanted with someone who worked for me. But your guy does a surprising thing. He doesn't call. He goes to see my guy with another guy and they do a gangster act on him."

"What guy is this?"

"Elmore."

"Oh, shit." Sal made a face.

"You didn't know this?"

"Elmore is always doing stuff on his own. I gotta put up with it. He's the idiot nephew of some guy I owe. I don't know what this is but I'll make it good. I don't mess with you, Fox, and you know that."

"You never did before."

"Each to his own," Sal said.

Fox thought about that. Drover had guessed right. Sal Marconi had nothing to do with this.

"Well, the idiot passed my guy an envelope that purports to show illegal bet slips—"

"Not from me."

"Not from you. Supposed to be people in Chicago."

"And?"

"He wants the guy—my guy—to get this third guy in trouble with his employers. Show the slips around. Act as the guy in the middle."

"What guys are we talking about?"

"Sal, I don't know and I don't want to know."

"Foxy, you forgive me." His voice was rendered soft to show there was no hard feeling behind what he was about to say. "You're full of shit. You come to this end of town to talk to me, so talk."

"I don't want any part of this. Neither does my guy. But he doesn't want a comeback from Elmore or his partner, whoever he was. He just wants it in your lap."

"Is that right?"

"I did a favor for Elmore because he indicated it was a favor for you."

"And why would you do me a favor?"

"Because I wanted to see what it was. That you would ask of someone who works for me. I don't put my head in the sand."

The 7-Up came and he took it. He tasted it to get the bad taste out of his mouth. He said words like *guy* for the benefit of Sal Marconi, not because he used words like that. You had to hit Sal over the head with a two-by-four, not to get his attention but to make him listen to you with a little respect. It was hard enough to stay on the square in a town that the Outfit founded but you could do it if you were careful. Fox was a careful man.

"So what do you want?"

"I would like you to see my guy."

"Who is your guy?"

"You'll know him."

Sal let it pass.

"That's it," Fox said.

"That's it? You come over here and tell me this and that's it? You want me to do a favor for your guy, is that it?"

"That's it."

"And you don't want to know nothing."

"I don't want to know nothing. And I don't want you to ever send Elmore over to see me again because I wouldn't believe he came from you."

"I understand that. That makes me mad, that Elmore would use my name in vain."

Fox let that pass.

"So, who you like with the Lakers and Bulls?" This was to signal the end of the previous conversation.

"Bulls by three."

"Generous man."

"You got them at four."

"Stir the pot. I heard something."

"I don't want to know."

"OK, Fox. I understand. I appreciate the respect you show me to come yourself on this errand." It was a tremendous expenditure of politeness for Sal, and Fox noted the gesture.

He finished the drink and put it on the coaster and got up. He even shook Sal's hand. Hopefully, no one was taking pictures.

"I will talk to your guy whenever."

"I'll send him right over."

"Not here. Tell him to meet me in the sports book at the Hilton. At midnight."

And Fox understood that as well. Elmore might be in a little trouble with Sal before this night was over.

But Fox didn't want to know about it.

TWENTY-THREE

W HEN FOX Vernon returned, he couldn't have been gone forty-five minutes. But Drover had disappeared. He asked his security man if Drover had left a message. The security man handed him a sealed envelope.

The message was scrawled on a single sheet of paper:

"Thanks for the favor. Now we're even. I quit. D."

He just stood and stared at it. The security man wanted to know if anything was wrong. Then he looked up and crumpled the sheet of paper at the same time. He tried a thin smile. But he didn't say anything.

The losers flight back to Chicago was a somber affair. The two-day junketeers had gambled their brains out for a frantic forty-eight hours and now they looked like denizens of a drunk tank on the morning after. Their eyes were blurred and their faces were ashen. They were leaving the land without clocks for time in the real world. Drover sometimes thought the slot players and 21 addicts and roulette mamas liked to make these quickies to Vegas with the same philosophy as the guy who bangs his head against a brick wall: It feels so much better when he stops.

The flight attendants were in a surly mood. Red-eye flights do that to the hired help. Drover tried to be inconspicuous. He sipped a vodka-something while reading *Sports Illustrated* by the night-light. When the words registered empty on his brain, he turned off the light, closed his eyes, and wondered how the human body, controlled by the human imagination, could go to sleep in an aluminum coffin at 39,000 feet. It turned out, as usual, to be easy.

Chicago was cold and cloudy on this April morning. O'Hare Airport was still full of sleep and as grouchy as any old man awakened by an alarm. The losers' night flight nosed into a jetway and let the players stumble off into the terminal. Drover felt as lousy as any of them.

He shivered in the cab line. Chicago can get so cold so fast that a native son who has lived too long in California forgets how thin his blood has become.

The Yellow came up and he climbed in. They took the Kennedy Expressway south and east toward downtown. The clouds cut off the tops of the Hancock Building and Sears Tower and the streets were damp.

He was too early to check in to the Drake Hotel. Besides, it was always better to do the unpleasant things first.

He had picked up Homer White's address from his buddy, Neil O'Neill at ESPN. O'Neill had been the b-ball coach at St. Mary's in Indiana and he and Drover had come to know each other too well over a matter of a St. Mary's scandal. The surprising turnout was that they liked each other. Enough for Neil to spin his Rolodex for Drover via long-distance telephone.

"Is there something I should know about Homer?" Neil said after giving out the number.

"His pins hurt."

"I know, I heard that. If his legs hurt any more, he'd be hitting .400," Neil said. "I can't sympathize with someone tearing up the league. He was on our show the other night. His charming self. He was sober and even mildly coherent. I thought he was almost human."

"Hell, Neil, sometimes I think you're almost human."

It was just six thirty in the morning and traffic was still light on Lake Shore Drive outside the high rise where Homer White paid $2,500 a month to sleep.

Drover paid the cabbie and crossed the sidewalk to the entrance. The doorman was watching him from his desk inside the lobby. When he entered, the doorman stared at him but didn't say anything.

"Homer White," Drover said.

"He expecting you?"

"Tell him it's Mr. Drover."

The doorman dialed a number and waited. Then he repeated the name. Then he handed the telephone to Drover.

"Whaddaya want?" Homer White said.

"I have to see you."

"I thought I tol' you once already to disappear."

"This is bad for you, Homer. I want to warn you."

"You gonna warn me what?"

"About Mae."

Silence.

Drover let the silence work.

"Warn me what about Mae?"

"Let me up?"

"No . . . I got someone here."

"I'll take five minutes. You can close the bedroom door. It's that important, I flew all the way here just to see you."

"You flew out here for this?"

"Come on, Homer."

"Why would you wanna do that?"

"There's a way to find out."

"All right. Gimme Hector on the door."

Drover handed back the phone and Hector, still keeping his eye on Drover, listened. Then he hung up the receiver and led the way to the inner door and opened it. "Apartment fourteen-oh-one."

The inner lobby was cold and empty, straight copy of Bauhaus in which an infinite number of rats are kept in identical sterile cages.

Buildings like this reminded Drover of institutions he didn't like to be reminded of. Like the buildings where G people worked.

Fourteen-oh-one was at the end of a gray-carpeted hall. The door was opening before he got there.

Homer was wearing a robe over his nakedness. His eyes were clear, boyish blue, and his blond hair was tousled from sleep. He didn't look friendly.

Drover carried his overnight bag through the door and Homer closed it quietly behind him. He said, "Keep your voice down. She's sleeping."

Drover sat on a modern steel-and-leather chair by the window wall. The lake below looked awfully cold and the gray of the day enhanced a feeling that the world would end before noon.

"I dunno why I let you up."

"Because you knew I wouldn't go away."

Homer sat down heavily on the couch opposite the leather chair. They had a glass coffee table between them. Drover looked around. The apartment was severe and as homey as a hospital waiting room.

"You decorate this yourself?"

"I rent it, asshole. What've you got in the bag?"

Drover unzipped the top of the bag and pulled out the brown envelope. He handed it to Homer.

Homer opened it.

He looked at the Xerox pages.

Then he looked at the photograph. He stared at the photograph a long time. Then he looked at Drover. "This is shit, you know."

"I know."

"I don't even know these guys."

"I know," Drover said.

"You say that, but you weren't that sure before."

"I know," Drover said.

"Don't keep saying you know. Tell me how you know."

"I was talking to people yesterday afternoon and someone said something about this and it made me take another look at the contents of the envelope. Then I saw it. I didn't see it before."

"See what?"

Drover pointed at the photograph.

"You. Look at you. You've got a scar on your cheek. That was since the accident. So this picture had to be made in the last eighteen months. Except you were in the hospital for two of those months and then on crutches and then you went into rehab. You didn't even join the team until July and then you said you were still getting rehabbing because of the arthritis or whatever it is that developed. So this picture had to be made in the last six months. And you told me you were a changed man. I finally remembered the name you gave me. Helen. Just Helen. That's your girlfriend, isn't it?"

"That ain't your business, asshole," Homer White said.

"Is it Mae's?"

"Mae knows I know this therapist. I tole her."

"Told her you love her, want to marry her?"

"No."

"When you going to tell her?"

"Isn't that my business?"

"I was talking to two women. They said I got it all wrong. I thought this move on you was connected to Max Heubner and it really isn't. This is about Mae. Mae wants something out of you that I don't understand but it has to do with your change in life status. You don't drink any more, like you said. You were a thirsty soldier in the old days, Homer. So was I. But you're a changed man. I talked to a couple of people about you. You don't drink and carouse anymore. It could be your legs. How are your legs?"

"You are the nosiest son of a bitch I ever met."

"Tell me about Mae. You tell Mae you want to go to Seattle?"

"Yeah."

"She said she'd help you?"

"Yeah."

"That's nice. What have you got that Mae wants?"

"I pay her alimony. She's working in real estate out in See City but I still pay her money every quarter. She's got no complaints."

"What about your daughter?"

"She's got no complaints neither."

Drover shook his head then. The brick wall was still there and he was still banging his head against it. At least the losers on the red-eye were all home by now, suiting up for their reality checks.

"Why would Mae want to do you a favor after all these years? I mean, she told me she was a friend of Heubner's and they did business together. Why would she go to bat for you?"

"Why not? When I was hurt, she come down to Caswell to see if I was hurting."

"No. You said to see if you were dying. That's what you told me."

"That wasn't well said. I was feeling in a mean spirit then."

"No. You said it like it was true."

"Well, we don't talk all that much. I mean, I ain't seen Mae except when she came to the hospital for ten, twelve years. We ain't close."

"What'd she talk to you about in the hospital."

"This and that. You know. We talked about Millie some. Then she said that if anything happened to me was Millie provided for and I tole her that I had a will and I was giving everything to Millie. My agent drew it up for me. You know, I tole her she didn't have to worry about that."

"Unless you get married again."

"Say what?"

"You are trying to keep it secret in your own loudmouth way but there are vibes around that you fell in love with your physical therapist. Don't blush, it happens all the time."

"I ain't blushing, but I might pop you one again."

"Don't. I've had a concussion on your behalf and four broken ribs that are currently making it hard for me to laugh."

"What concussion?"

"Max Heubner took exception to some things I said to him a couple of days ago."

"You had it coming probably."

"Probably."

"Well, why you want to warn me about Mae? Mae's in Seattle."

"Mae wants you in Seattle too. And the other scenario is that they want you out of Chicago and out of baseball. Whatever it takes to make it work. One day I get two goons telling me that I should pass on to the press the information in that envelope about you gambling. Next day, I get a call from your wife saying I should work on Eddie Briggs to trade you to the Mariners so you can live out your old age in baseball as a DH. That is a very amateur production and it struck me that way at the time but I was looking for the Machiavelli in the wrong place. It isn't Heubner. It's your ex-wife. She wants you in her clutches or she wants you out of the limelight, one or the other."

"And why would she want that?"

"Because she's afraid you're going to get married and change your will."

The statement left both of them breathless and blinking. Drover wouldn't know how he came to the words any more than he could explain the act of writing on a laptop Zenith in a no-name hotel in downtown See City. Sometimes if you worried around a thing long enough, it just came naturally.

"I put my goddamned farm up for sale and when the day comes that Helen says yes, then, by God, I am getting married again." He growled this. "And that's none of your business and none of Mae's business. And by God, I'm gonna tear a new asshole through the National fucking League this year that is gonna make Eddie Briggs a rich man, trading away ole Homer for some bright young pitchers from the AL. Now whaddaya think of that?"

"Captain Courageous," Drover said. "But why would Eddie trade you if you did good? You're not reasoning this out. If he holds a grudge against you for screwing his wife—"

"Who tole you I ever was involved with his wife?"

"Heubner," Drover said. No point in going over the ground raked by the U.S. attorney.

"How's that son of a bitch know that?"

"I would guess it came from Mae."

"Damn."

"You did tell Mae once, didn't you?"

"Damn."

"See, Homer? What goes around comes around. You were a bad boy for a lot of years and now you're paying for your sins. You got enemies, boy."

Homer shook his head. It was a slow and sad shake. The window wall rattled in the wind. Cold and gray light made the apartment dingy.

"But I ain't gonna die," Homer said in a weak voice.

"We're all going to die, Homer. Some of us get hurried into it.

Max Heubner is a bad man, a very bad man. My guess is that he knows that man in the photo. That's Mr. Ricci, Mr. Tony Ricci of the local Outfit. I figure that Mr. Ricci, for unknown reasons, does not want to knock off a member of the Chicago Cubs in his hometown. It is called not shitting where you sleep. Besides, you've been a good boy. You don't gamble and whore around anymore since you've found God."

"Don't make fun of this. I ain't found God yet but I'm looking for Him."

"Same thing," Drover said. "I guessed this photo was a fake. I took it over to a friend who runs the photography department at the University of California at Santa Cruz. He guesses it's a fake too, at least your part in the photo. So I have to guess as well.

"Max Heubner has Vegas connections because he uses Mob money in his building schemes. He gets an idiot named Elmore Leonardo and another idiot—the middle guy in that photo—to set you up on the gambling stuff. Maybe the idea was that if it all got out about you gambling, he could get Mr. Ricci to have you snuffed in Chicago as the Cub who went bad. Maybe not. Maybe you'd just be banned from baseball and go home to Arkansas. Where you could be whacked just as easy because you would then be a nobody. Or maybe he could lure you to Seattle where Heubner might just snuff you himself or, maybe, get you back together with Mae, anything to keep you from your Chicago girlfriend or from getting married. Or from changing your will."

"That is just wild-eyed shit. You shoulda been a Sherlock Holmes or something, boy, you are making this shit up."

"Yeah. Except I was in the middle of it. It didn't make sense to me. They wanted to use me because I was down on you. Who remembers that you made a deposition to the G about me ten years ago? That I was a loose character and went around with immoral people in my salad days? Who remembers that shit? Nobody. Certainly, Heubner wouldn't know it. But Mae would know. And Tony Ricci would know because the gangsters I allegedly consorted with were from Chicago. That's the only way I could have gotten involved in this. It was a reach. Like I said, this thing was amateur from the start but that doesn't mean it wasn't dead on. And you started the pot boiling by mentioning you had a girlfriend in Chicago. Helen whoever she is."

"Helen Brown."

The woman came out of the bedroom. She was tall and she wore a white terry-cloth robe over her nightgown. Her hair was tousled by sleep and she wore no makeup. She was beautiful.

"Helen Brown. Miss Brown," Drover said and he felt compelled to rise.

"How do you do? Mr. Drover? Do you have a first name?"

"Jimmy."

"Mr. Drover," she said and extended her hand.

Homer had risen as well.

"This don't involve you, Helen."

"Sure it does. Mr. Drover is making that clear, Homeboy."

Drover smiled.

Miss Brown caught it and returned it then, a soft smile that was edged with sad lines. "I'm sorry, Homer."

"You've heard, then?" Drover said.

"You boys talk in very loud voices when you say you're whispering."

"I'm sorry, Honey. This is not going to come back to you, I swear to God, is it, Drover?"

"No. I don't want it to come back to anyone. That's why I put the fix in last night on Elmore and his partner. I think they will be disciplined. I think Heubner will be taken care of in the bye and bye. But there's still Homer and I couldn't sleep at night if I didn't warn him."

"He's full of shit, Helen, don't listen to him."

"Be quiet, Homer," she said then. She sat down on the couch and the men decided to sit as well. She looked at the Xerox sheets and at the photograph.

Drover looked at her.

He had not expected her to be black.

What a strange sense of humor God has, he thought. Homer White of all people. And a beautiful black woman named Helen Brown.

They waited for her to finish. When she put down the photograph at last, she clasped her hands on her knees and spoke to Drover.

"Why warn him about Mae?"

He hesitated. It was only a feeling. He remembered Mae in the Italian restaurant. She treated him like an errand boy. Maybe it was just a feeling that he couldn't explain about the way she talked, the way she spun out her lies, about her sudden rage and just as sudden violence. Maybe it was nothing. Except it all came together when Nancy said she was the center of everything and said it in her hard voice with her tight little smile.

"Mae. You told Mae you were selling the farm in Arkansas."

"No, I was getting round to it."

"You tell anyone?"

"Told you just now. Told Helen. Told Buddy Gooch cause he's selling it for me. That's all. And Millie, my daughter, told her."

"Millie close to her mom?"

"Closer'n two ticks on a boll weevil. That's been a good thing. I wasn't close to Millie but I been trying to make up for it. Helen here had a close family and she made me see that family is somethin' you gotta work at."

"Homer, I'm close to voting for you if you're running," Drover said. He looked at Helen. "So Mae knows. And that signals something for Mae. Homer is selling the farm, something's up. You're not going back to Arkansas in the off season, are you, Homer?"

"You know so goddamned much about me, why don't you just write the story of my future life, which saves me the trouble of living it?"

"Homer," she said.

"Would Heubner do it? For Mae?" Drover was asking himself.

"Do what?"

"We have three scenarios. Trade to Seattle. Get you banned from baseball. Or whack you and to hell with the publicity that would create. I mean, Al Capone did whack Jack Lingle."

"I dunno what you talkin' about."

"The rules are you don't whack the press. Lingle was a newspaper reporter. In my kind of town."

"What's he talking about, Honey?"

"I know."

Drover looked at her hard. She did know.

"He can take the farm off the market," Helen said. "I won't see him anymore."

"Wait a minute, Helen."

"It might work," Drover said. "It might be too late. If it weren't you, it might be someone else. Maybe Mae has been drifting along, just figuring that along the way she'd get hers. Through her daughter. And then you want to sell this farm? Is it worth anything?"

"Wasn't worth spit in a bucket of warm beer afore two years ago when Caswell come to life. The Japanese, goddamned Japs, come to Caswell to build their funny little cars. People down to Caswell couldn't be happier if they was twins. It's disgusting but that's no never mind. Bidness is bidness and those people want to sell to the Japs, then I can sell my farm. Hell, yes, my farm is worth ten times all of a sudden what I paid for it. Housing developers want—"

He just stopped talking.

"Heubner Construction," Drover said.

"I dunno no names."

"Ole Buddy Gooch down in Caswell might."

"You mean Buddy is part of this too?"

"No, I don't think we have to reach that conclusion. It's just that real estate is real estate. Like a car dealer I knew once in the Valley. He explained that the secret to selling used cars and getting the most out of trade-ins is always being on the lookout for someone looking for a certain type of vehicle and then combing new customers for new cars to see if they have that kind of car to trade. If Buddy Gooch is in real estate, he might just know more about real estate prices round Caswell today than you do. Not that he's cheating you, I didn't say that. I said, you got property that's worth something and you're selling it. Mae thinks you're selling it because you're not going home. She thinks you're not going home because you're going to get married and live up north. And that means it's all come to a head right now."

"So I can stop seeing Homer," Helen began again.

Drover held up his hand. "You don't have to. I'm going to work on a trade for Homer."

"Trade?"

"See if we can get you into the AL. You going to be able to play this year?"

"I can play. Hit eight home runs already."

"I know, but it's early." He was looking at Helen again.

"He's found his courage that was there all along. It was just buried a little," she said. "He's one of the great baseball players and if it takes pain, he'll pay it."

She had never said such a thing to Homer. He was amazed to hear it. And he squeezed her then and kissed her on the cheek and she let him.

"Damn," Drover said.

"Ah can't go back to Arkansas. Not at least to my little corner of it. Caswell ain't Little Rock. Not that we're too prejudiced now, it just takes time for people to learn and I don't want Helen to ever have one bad day. Besides, I like the big city. I really do. I like all those funny little restaurants, eating that foreign stuff. You get tired of chicken-fried steaks. Never really saw the city until I was with Helen and she made me see it. I used to think it was just Rush Street and feeling up those lollypops after a game. It's a nice old city and more important, it ain't prejudiced like we are down in Caswell."

"Come on, Homeboy, I never said that." But she was smiling at him, holding his hand. Drover thought it looked like love and something else. Maybe it was love and happiness. They so rarely went together.

"Well, you keep the envelope, Homer. No one saw it except me. And a friend of mine who isn't ever going to tell anyone. The guys who gave it to me will be disciplined in their own way. I've got miles to go today, people to see, you know. So keep your head down, Homer. For a few days. This is all going to work out."

Helen said, "Is it?"

"Sure," Drover lied. He didn't have the faintest idea.

TWENTY-FOUR

T HE NEXT stop was in River Forest.

It is a suburb west of Chicago with high taxes, wide lawns, and elegant homes, along with the occasional mansion. Lawyers live here and sometimes the people certain lawyers represent. People like Tony Rolls.

Tony Rolls was a retired mobster with wheels turned into atrophied muscle. He used a wheelchair all the time and never grumbled about it. He had has mansion and he had poker games and he had his attendants, Vin and Rocco. He ate pasta, drank red wine, and every now and then he amused himself in other ways.

Like granting an audience to Jimmy Drover.

He had known Jimmy as a kid on the West Side. The West Side was always a melting pot of ethnics and races who got along as long as they had to. Drover, unlike his honorary uncle Tony, had no bent for bending the law. His mother raised him right, and his other honorary uncle was a police captain. Cops and crooks and lawyers between them came out of the old neighborhood. It was the kind of place where people sat on the stoops on warm summer nights and kept an eye on everyone's kid playing in the streets. Still is, in parts.

Drover took a cab out because he knew that Tony Rolls would like to show off his power by ordering one of his cars and drivers to take Drover back to wherever he wanted to go.

He brought along a bottle of Orvieto that had cost $40. Tony Rolls would know the price. He was a cripple but he was many other things, including a connoisseur of things you digest. He had picked up the name of Tony Rolls from the rolls of quarters he had once used to fatten his fists.

Drover was taken into the parlor by Vin, who frowned as much as possible at the visitor. Drover gave Tony the bottle of wine and Tony looked at it and nodded. He was pleased. He might have three cases of the same stuff in the cellar but it was a mark of respect.

When Vin left them, Drover began. He took his time because it was a complicated story. He left out the part about Helen being a black woman. Maybe he still didn't believe it. Not Homer White.

"So," Tony said at last, "you know I'm retired from whatever it was I used to do."

"I understand. I don't want to be involved in anything and I don't want to see the people in your business here get involved in anything bad. Homer is no connection to your people at all. He used to gamble but he paid up his debts long ago."

"I hear his pins are hurting him. He should take care of himself so he don't end up like me."

"He does. The woman in his life puts him through his paces."

"That's good. Women are very good at making us take care of ourselves. I think men would not even live as long as we do if it wasn't for women. I miss my wife very much. I think of her every day and I light a candle in church for her every Sunday at mass. She was such a good woman to put up with me."

He had tears in his eyes. Part of Tony Rolls's life now was crying at unexpected moments when he thought of the few tender things that had ever been part of his past.

"God rest her soul," Drover said. He remembered her as a butterball of a woman constantly making spaghetti sauce, stirring the pot over and over, and teaching little boys like Drover how to say the Hail Mary in Italian.

"I can see where these amateurs might go off half cocked. I mean, it is very legitimate business that some of our people are involved in, the real estate business, construction also, but then you should work it as a business and not go and get involved in some plot by some people who are not even in this environment. Is that what you think, Drover?"

"I think that."

"But." He held up his hands and let them drop. "But it's not my concern. I can't give you any advice."

"You could give Mr. Ricci advice."

"Why would he listen to me?"

"Because Mr. Heubner is not good for him to be with."

"Why is that?"

Drover stared at Tony Rolls for a long time. He thought about the cracked ribs still encased in bandages under his shirt. This one was for the Gipper.

"Because the G is going to dump on Mr. Heubner very soon."

Tony Rolls sat still.

"Do you know this thing?" His growl was as quiet as a midnight El train rattling through an abandoned neighborhood. He sat very still in his wheelchair, his head cocked to the side, waiting.

"Perhaps." And Drover put his finger to his lips.

"I understand," Tony Rolls said. "Well, that would be very good advice to give someone like Anthony Ricci and he would probably listen to it."

"Yes, if it came from the right source."

"As you said. The right source. I'm an old man but an old man hears many things."

"But the original source is a secret."

"Of course. Do you think I'd want people to know I would talk to people like you?"

Drover blinked.

Tony laughed then, his belly shaking out sounds through his mouth. Joke. It was a Tony Rolls joke. What a card. Drover smiled in return while the old man laughed. And thought of Heubner, who wouldn't have seen the humor of this at all.

TWENTY-FIVE

THE BELLMAN placed the single suitcase on the suitcase rack near the door and turned on the lights in the john and made sure the television worked.

Al Pardee let him go through his show and then fished a couple of dollars out of his pocket and passed them to the man in uniform. The bellman handed him a key card and let himself out.

Al Pardee sat down on the edge of the bed and turned on the television set. It was Oprah Winfrey time of the morning. He stared at her and didn't see her at all. He was seeing Drover. He always saw Drover now, everywhere, in every face. There was a guy on the plane who looked exactly like Drover, so much so that Al Pardee had to look twice.

Al Pardee was running and he didn't like running and he didn't like the thought that Drover was doing this to him.

Ten years later and Drover was still doing it to him.

He had barely known the geek in Los Angeles days. One guy mentioned his name once, said he was originally from Chicago, that when he grew up he knew Tony Rolls, who was a big shot in those days in Chicago. That's all he knew about the guy and yet, somehow, the guy had managed to do him in so that he ended up doing three years in federal prison. Sure, he was guilty, but that wasn't the point. Someone had snitched on him, and when the assistant U.S. attorney told him it was Drover, he couldn't believe it.

It took him three years in prison to believe it. Three years of days and nights, thinking about Drover. And when he finally got paroled, it was with all kinds of conditions. Like working for the G still but from inside the environment. All because of a geek named Drover.

Was it any wonder that Drover drove Al Pardee crazy?

Al got up then, snapped off the TV, and went to his bag. He opened the bag and removed the object wrapped in black cloth. It was a pistol, a .9-mm Beretta semi-automatic with a black silencer attachment. The pistol took a fourteen-shot clip.

The night before, Leonardo had called him in Seattle. Told him that Sal Marconi wanted to see him about the thing that he and Leonardo had done in Seattle. Trying to sic Drover on Homer White. Elmore Leonardo sounded scared and that made Al Pardee scared. Al Pardee packed in a hurry and took a cab the long ride south to the Seattle-Tacoma airport. His first thought was to go to Chicago, see his pals, hide out a while. His second thought was more rational. He was still on parole. He had to check in with the U.S attorney first.

Drover had somehow managed to sic Sal Marconi onto Leonardo, and Leonardo, to do himself a favor, sicced his boss onto Al Pardee. This whole thing, the thing of working for the U.S. attorney putting together an indictment on Max Heubner—the whole thing could blow up in Al Pardee's face.

He looked into the mirror on the vanity and studied his face. Studied his big, fat features and small piggy eyes. Studied the prison pallor that he could not shake after six years outside. Studied the shape of his huge, slumping shoulders.

That fucking geek Drover. How did he get leverage with Sal Marconi to put the fear on Leonardo and then make Leonardo put the fear on Pardee? It just went to prove how connected Drover was, how Drover could have gotten him three years in prison in the first place.

He called the U.S. Attorney from the Sea-Tac airport. Frank Chesrow was not pleased that Al Pardee, his number-one snitch, was leaving for a quick vacation in Chicago.

"This isn't some more bullshit about this Drover guy, is it?" Frank Chesrow said.

That had startled Pardee, who began to stammer the first lie that came into his head. But Chesrow cut him short. "We've been keeping tabs on Drover. He went to Vegas briefly and then to Chicago."

"How do you know these things?" Pardee said.

"We watch credit cards," Chesrow said, showing off.

"You mean Drover is in Chicago?"

"I told you, lay off this Drover thing. I don't want you to go to Chicago. I don't want to hear about Drover or baseball or nothing but what we're working on, which is Max Heubner," Chesrow said.

"All right," Pardee had said. Suddenly. Standing in the airport, talking on a pay phone, smiling suddenly.

"All right what?"

"All right. I won't go to Chicago," Pardee had said. "I'll go down to L.A. for a couple of days instead. I just got to get away."

"You stay in touch, Al."

"I'll stay in touch."

He charged the flight to L.A. on American Express so that Frank Chesrow would see that he had gone there. Then he paid cash for a ticket from Los Angeles to Chicago.

At LAX, he called his friend Ricci in Chicago. Before he could say anything, Ricci said it for him. "I dunno what beef you got going for you with this guy Drover but I don't want no part of it," Ricci said.

"No part of what?"

"Whatever you got going for you, I don't wanna know," Ricci said.

What the hell was going on? Pardee was standing in the terminal in LAX and reaching out to Ricci in Chicago and Ricci, even Ricci, was reciting the magic name: Drover. Drover. Drover. The guy had tentacles everywhere.

Ricci hung up on him in mid-sentence. His buddy.

Fucking Drover. Who was this guy, Superman?

It worked on him on the four-hour flight east to Chicago. It worked on him during the twenty-seven-dollar cab ride to the Intercontinental Hotel on Michigan Avenue. It worked on him now, in his hotel room, staring at his fat face in the mirror, thinking about how he was going to deal with Drover once and for all.

He turned from the mirror and sat down at the desk. He opened the phone book and began to dial numbers. The sixth hotel was the Drake. Just up the street. Yes, sir, Mr. Drover, the switchboard operator said and switched him to Drover's room.

He hung up. Drover was in the Drake Hotel.

He got up, went back to the weapon on the television table. He picked it up and pointed it at his image in the mirror.

"Pow," he said. "Pow, pow."

Fuck Heubner, fuck the feds, fuck Chesrow, fuck Leonardo, fuck Ricci, fuck Homer White and doing Heubner a favor to get him out to Seattle. Fuck everything right now but Drover. Drover was what he wanted and what he was going to get.

Pow, pow.

TWENTY-SIX

M<small>AE TILSON</small> also had a gun.

And she was also in Chicago.

Unlike Al Pardee, she had never seen anyone's federal file. She didn't need one.

She looked so strange on the plane from Seattle that the flight attendants kept asking her if she wanted anything. She kept saying no. She just sat by herself in the back of the plane and thought about things. The more she thought, the madder she got.

At the airport she took a cab to Elmwood Park, to an address on Mannheim Road.

The address turned out to be a gun shop. She knew it from the days when she and Homer were first living in the Chicago area and they had heard all those terrible stories and she and Homer had bought her a pistol to keep at home and keep her safe.

The guy was only too glad to sell her another pistol. Then she ordered up a cab to take her into town.

When she got into Chicago, the cab dropped her at the Palmer

House in the Loop and she registered under her own name. She didn't care now who knew. She had to do something and she was the only one who could do it. So it just had to be done, like cleaning up a dirty bathroom or washing down the walls. It just had to be done. Men were not going to screw her around anymore, not Max, not Homer, not any man.

She was led to her room by the bellman, who asked her if she needed anything. He sounded just like the flight attendants had sounded. She practically snapped a *no* but she gave him two dollars as a tip.

She wasn't really thinking clearly beyond the next thing, which was to get the no-good son of a bitch and his no-good fucking girlfriend.

Not just a girlfriend, that was bad enough. But she was black. Black, for God's sake. That had snapped it finally for Mae, when Millie mentioned that Helen Brown was a black woman.

A black hooker, some black hooker he'd picked up after the game or something. Homer was going to marry a black whore and give her everything? That was the last thing that was going to happen.

She had found out when she called Millie, when she was still wavering a little about doing what had to be done, like putting off cleaning up the mess in the bathroom. She had called Millie because she called Millie all the time to ask her how she was doing in school and Millie had said that Daddy was going to marry an African-American woman and wasn't that the neatest, wildest thing?

The neatest, wildest thing?

The fuck it was.

She was so crazy now that people parted for her when she walked down the sidewalk in her fur coat and slacks, just glowering ahead like a locomotive with a blinding light in her killer eyes.

It mattered to Mae because she just hated blacks, and this one, this Helen, she was cutting herself in on Homer just when Mae thought it was set. Homer had gone through girls all those years and never lasted more than a few weeks with one. And now this colored broad had flipped him to the point where he was selling the farm and when they got married—married!—she would become his heir. Cutting out Millie, poor little Millie.

State Street was full of people shopping, going to work, begging at the sidelines. HOMELESS AND BLIND said one sign and JESUS BLESS YOU said another. Fur coats and rags mingled on the wide walks and Mae didn't see any of this as she strode along. She didn't even know where she was going; she just had to keep moving or the energy of anger in her would explode. She was walking fast, her cheeks inflamed, her hard eyes directed at nothing but her thoughts. Thinking about how she was going to do it.

That's what people saw as she strode down the street to the taxi stand in front of the hotel. Killer eyes.

TWENTY-SEVEN

DROVER LET Vin drive him back to the Drake Hotel from River Forest. Vin was his usual uncommunicative self all the way.

Vin was the color of a football and his skin seemed to be pebbled like one. Baiting him was harmless as long as you were under the protection of Tony Rolls.

When they reached the Drake, Vin spent a couple of dimes off his clip of words to tell Drover he was an asshole. Drover said he knew that already.

When Vin was gone, Drover went into the hotel and rented a car. It pulled up outside fifteen minutes later. He studied a map of Chicago and suburbs and decided on the best way to get to Lake Forest.

Lake Forest is one of those rich towns that pretends it is something more than a suburb of a sprawling metropolis. It sniffs its collective nose at both the city south of it and the less classy suburbs around it.

The house was set back in trees and it was near the lakefront. Lake Forest has a college and it has money. People who run Chicago live in places like Lake Forest.

The name on the mailbox at the rustic curb read BRIGGS.

It was early afternoon and the morning clouds had given way to sunshine. It was the kind of baseball day that used to make Ernie Banks say, "Let's play two." Fortunately for Homer's legs, the Cubs were only playing one with the Brewers and a big right-hander named Smoking Joe Robinson was on the mound for Milwaukee. The Cubs were favored because the wind was blowing out in the bandbox park. Wrigley Field is to pitchers what hell is to sinners.

Drover rang the bell twice and then went around to the back. She was on the deck, catching the thin rays of the afternoon sun. There was a pool too, but it was too cold to use it. She wore a sleeveless top and white shorts and she was very pretty. Just the kind of gal that Homer White might commit adultery with.

"Hello."

She started.

"My name is Drover, Miz Briggs. I'm a friend of Homer White."

"What do you want? My husband just went to the drugstore— he'll be right back." She was on her feet and there was a glass pitcher of something dark in her hand.

Drover stood still. When confronting strange dogs or frightened women, stand still. Don't let them know you're as afraid as they are.

"What do you want?"

"My name is Drover. I'm a writer. I'm doing a book on famous adulterers. You know, Lord Nelson, Vita Sackville-West, John F. Kennedy. The whole gamut. I know Homer White and I know about you and Homer White from a long time ago."

"I'll call a policeman."

"Look. I'll get off your property. I just thought it was easier this way if I told you what was happening instead of talking to you and your husband at the same time or going to the president of the Cubs with it."

That eased her a little but she still held the pitcher in her hand. Drover said, "Can I sit down?"

"You stay over there."

"I will."

He waited. She waited. She edged toward the patio door. He stood still. She opened the door and stood in the frame of the door.

"All right," he said. "Stay there or go in the house if you want. I just want to tell you something that you can act on. That Eddie can act on."

"Tell what?"

"Homer White. About what happened in Little Rock a long time ago."

"That was a long time ago. Why would Homer bring that up now?"

"He didn't exactly. I brought it up. The book I'm writing. It's called *In Someone Else's Bed.* I'm trying to decide if the first serial rights will go to the *Star* or *Vanity Fair.*"

"I don't know what you're talking about."

"Girl gets guy with roving eye. Girl gets even with another guy who roves as well. Girl and second guy look for love in all the wrong places. Girl gets back at first guy. I'll stop. I'm talking like a movie Indian. What it comes down to is that Homer had to explain to someone what happened once a long time ago in order to explain his predicament now."

"Homer's predicament?"

"Don't you know what it is, Lu Ann?"

She blinked in the sunlight. Her hair was fair and her skin was freckled already. She seemed so delicate, standing there in the patio doorway in bare feet, it was hard to believe she could have slugged it out against her husband using a big dope like Homer White.

"I'm sure I don't." The accent was going south in a hurry. It was in the Missouri Ozarks, heading for the Arkansas border. "I'm sure whatever it is, you're mistaken."

"Homer wants to be traded to the American League and your husband won't let him."

Another moment of tableau. And then she took a step onto the deck again. The pitcher was still in her hand.

"What's this about?"

"Eddie has a fine new career with the Cubs and they take care of their own. It's a solid franchise and they can fill the park most every day. Homer is on his last legs—you would notice that if you saw the way he plays outfield. But he can still hit."

"I don't care two cents for Homer White."

"You should. You took advantage of him. You cheated on your husband with him."

"It takes two to cheat."

"So it does. And it happened a long time ago." Drover said it slowly. "But what if Eddie held a grudge all this time and he was willing to use a crippled-up ballplayer, run him down instead of doing what was best for the team? Instead of dumping him off on some team in the AL that could use a solid DH in their lineup and wouldn't gulp at the price? I mean, six million is chicken feed for someone who's hitting like Homer. There was talk about getting him in the winter trade meets but your husband kept bad-mouthing Homer to the other GMs. That's not cricket. It's not even baseball. He's punishing you by keeping Homer around on a short leash, isn't he?"

There.

She put the pitcher down and took three more steps. She had left the patio door open.

"How do you know all this?"

"I have a friend in broadcasting who told me some of it. And I figured out some of it myself. And I don't think it's right. What Homer was and what he did is past. Bury the past. You want to bury it, I know that, Mrs. Briggs. But Eddie likes to keep bringing it up, doesn't he?"

"Eddie and I have worked out our problems."

"I'm sure. Happy marriages are made of compromises. But I think it would be better if you talked to Eddie when he comes home tonight. About how I know what he's doing and if I know, it'll get out. And then the president of the Cubs will know and he'll say that this is not a good thing and he'll be suspicious of everything Eddie does after that. That wouldn't help his career, would it?"

"You'd do that? Hurt Eddie? For that miserable redneck son of a bitch? He's from trash, nothin' but trash."

"Homer may have been a miserable bastard but he was good enough for you in Little Rock."

"It had nothing to do with him."

"I know. It had to do with Fast Eddie, didn't it?"

"You really writin' a book? About adultery?"

"Maybe not. It gets boring after a while. When it comes down to it, writing about the old in and out is a lot like writing about baseball. There are only so many ways to say it fresh."

"Eddie thought I was the only one who was married."

"Well, talk to him tonight."

"Why should I?"

"Because I give it a week at the most. In one week, I'll hear that Homer has been traded. Or I'll have a chat with the president of the team."

"Why would he talk to you?"

"I told you. I have a friend in broadcasting. He gets me in at private parties all the time. So he'd get me an audience with the president of the Cubs, I'm sure."

"This is blackmail, isn't it?"

Drover had thought about that all the way up to Lake Forest.

"Yes, it is. I know, I know, two wrongs don't make a right. But sometimes you just have to blunder along the best you can. You see? What Eddie is doing isn't right and what you did wasn't right and what Homer did wasn't right but sometimes we just have to learn to get along. We have to stop counting up the score and just say the game is finished and all go home."

She stared at him for a long time. There were songbirds in the trees all around them.

"You see?" he said.

"You're a lowlife, aren't you?"

"Guilty. I'm all things to all men. I was an asshole this morning."

"I can't say nothin' to rile you?"

"It's all been said by better rilers."

"I swear I didn't know—I don't know now—that Eddie is doing what you accuse him of doing. Homer is hittin' pretty good, ain't he?" The accent was in Little Rock and still heading south. Maybe it was sneaking around some of those suburban motels where she and Homer had made their beds years ago.

"Oh, Eddie's doing it, all right."

"What are you to Homer? His big brother? Guardian angel?"

"I was trying out for the second thing but I couldn't dance on the head of a pin."

"I don't know what you're saying."

"I don't know half the time myself. You going to talk to Eddie tonight?"

Another long pause in which they listened to the songbirds sing.

"I don't know what Eddie will do. What did you say your name was?"

"Drover. Mr. Drover. You think about what I told you, Lu Ann?" Jimmy Drover said.

"How can I not think about it? You just about ruined this afternoon for me," she said. "You come sneaking round the house, I won't be able to go out on the deck without thinking that someone'll come sneaking around."

"I didn't know any other way," he said.

"Homer shouldn't've told. Not to a stranger."

Drover turned then. He started off the deck and around the house and stopped. He looked back at her.

"Homer shouldn't have driven you home that night," Drover said.

TWENTY-EIGHT

I⊤ WAS a strange night in the city.

At sundown, clouds blew in from the northwest and the coming storm was announced by lightning across the sky. The Loop towers and those along Michigan Avenue were lit and people hurried to buses and subways and taxis, moving along smartly just ahead of the storm. When it came, it was huge, big wet drops plopping on the pavement and washing down to the gutters. Then came hail that rattled against the plate-glass windows of all the stores. If you didn't have a home to go home to in the city, it was the beginning of a bad night. The homeless huddled under the viaducts and under Wacker Drive and listened to the wet sounds and the thunder above them. The cardboard housing stained as water found its way to the underground from the pavements above. Booze and drugs eased the primitive fear and silenced the God voices at the edge of demented minds. In the aboveground city, the streets were swept with headlamps and despair. Laughter in the joints along Hubbard and Halsted streets was nervous, on edge. Everything was on edge.

Drover sat in his hotel room for a long time just brooding about everything.

He felt bad because there was no good anyplace. The despair was in the bright desk lamp, on the muted television screen where a news anchor pronounced the day's toll.

Homer White had drawn the world to him the way the storm was drawn to the city. Homer had stepped out of his old skin and put on a new man and it didn't matter because he had left such wreckage behind. A wrecked marriage and a woman who wanted to steal from him because it belonged to her for the suffering and abandonment she had gone through.

Thunder and lightning. God is moving his furniture, his mother used to say. Even God was cleaning house. Maybe God was on edge as well.

Eddie Briggs and Lu Ann Briggs, who had patched it back together but still held out little hurts for each other. She had used Homer and Homer had used her.

Homer White praised the Lord and wanted to marry the decent woman who had caused all this mess in the first place.

Helen Brown. Let's blame it on the blameless. She had taken Homer in hand and saved his sorry-ass soul. But she couldn't do anything about the wreckage of the past, not at all. So why hadn't she left bad enough alone? Save one poor soul but what about the others drifting in the flood?

Thunder has depth along the canyon streets. Windows rattled and people went to bed early to hide under the covers.

Drover got up and went to the TV and stared down at the news anchors mouthing their tidings without sound. Who needed sound when it was always the same old thing?

Helen didn't want Homer to marry her because Homer would give her the things that another woman—Mae—claimed. Or maybe Helen didn't love him at all but took him out of pity. Christ, why involve Drover in all this?

And who was Mae to claim Homer after nearly twenty years? She had lived on his alimony and he had been faithful in that way. When could Homer stop paying?

And Heubner. Heubner involved with Mae and Heubner reach-

ing to Vegas for his connections and then dragging into this poor little
Jimmy Drover, who went up to Seattle to write a quickie book about
the coming NFL season.

Poor little Jimmy.

Poor everyone.

"Shit," Drover said.

He called Kelly in Santa Cruz. Kelly was out for the evening with
Nancy Harrington. It was all right. No message. Nothing urgent.

"Shit," Drover said.

He had to leave his room. He took the elevator down to the big
red Drake lobby and then the steps down to the front entrance. The
doorman whistled and cabs inched along in the cab line and they all
wanted to go to O'Hare. Fuck 'em.

Self-pity was going to squeeze the life out of him and he wasn't
going to stand for it. Self-pity was for losers. He wasn't going to lose.

Drover walked across the city in the rain and found a dry spot in
the Green Door Tavern on Orleans. He ordered supper and a drink.
He didn't feel like eating but he ate. He didn't feel anything.

And then he thought about the worst thing and that started the
feelings going again. The night outside settled into an ordinary rain.
God was finished cleaning house.

The worst thing was that Homer White deserved everything that
he might get, every bad thing he had stirred up in his sorry life.

TWENTY-NINE

Drover sat in the tavern for a long time, nursing a single glass of local beer, and watched the basketball game. The Knicks were muscling the Bulls and it was working. Over on the other screen, the White Sox were losing to the Yankees. New York was beating up Chicago all over the place and it was being carried on television.

He decided he had had enough sports about ten and got up to leave when a stranger next to him saved his life.

She was blond and had the manner of someone who runs a company or eats steak whenever and wherever she feels like it. She was past thirty and she drank beer.

The woman said, "I hate New York. Why can't we ever beat those guys?"

Drover smiled at her. The stranger smiled back. "I'm serious," she said. "I hate the Big Apple."

"Second City. We have to be Second City."

"Why is that?"

"I don't know," Drover said.

"The Bears. I quit on the Bears when they got rid of Ditka. Now what do I got? I got the Cubs, I still got the Cubs, but the Cubs ain't never gonna win nothing. I know that and they know that. I get going on the Sox and what happens? They lose to the Yankees. The stinking Yankees. I hate the Yankees."

"You've always got the Mets."

"And the Mets beat the Cubs in 1969 when the Cubs should of won the pennant. You see? It's always New York. I don't care what you say, it's a conspiracy."

Drover sat down. He wasn't thinking about Homer or Mae or Fox Vernon testing him or about Max Huebner beating his ribs up. He was thinking about this irrational us-versus-them argument. "You got the Bulls," he said.

"Da Bulls. The Knicks are killing them. The rest of the country, we gotta go by rules. New York's got no rules."

"Maybe that's it. No rules," Drover said.

"You're not one of them, are you?"

"What?"

"A New Yorker."

"No."

"Cuz I can usually tell. New Yorkers have a third eye in the middle of their foreheads. Usually, they keep it closed but sometimes they slip up and open it and reveal themselves."

"I'm from the West Side."

"That's all right then. Lana, get this West Side guy a beer and get me another beer."

That's the way it went.

One beer and then another and then a serious analysis of the Bulls and the Blackhawks and the Sox and the Cubs and the hapless Bears. A sobering analysis of New York sports teams and what was wrong with New York as a city. Drover even revealed that he lived in California now, but that could not get a rise out of her. She didn't hate California, only New York.

"What do you do?" Drover got around to after the second beer.

"I'm a speech therapist," she said. Her name was Ella.

"Really?"

"Of course not. I have lousy grammer when I watch sports. Or when I get mad, which is usually the same thing."

"What do you do?"

"I own a saloon," she said.

And it turned out she did but she never drank in it. Drover had never met a woman who owned a saloon in Chicago and said so. And she said when she was graduated from Northwestern, she discovered there were no jobs for new lawyers so she did the next best thing— open a saloon.

It went on like that for a couple of hours. Ella was funny and Drover let his damp spirit dry out in her company. When he thought it was time to hit on her, she saw it and said, "Don't ruin a beautiful friendship."

He grinned. And didn't.

They talked about sports and sports writing and New York and gambling in Vegas and he tried to be as interesting about himself as she was. Ella Mackey. He wouldn't even have to write her name down in a phone book.

Which is why Drover didn't leave the Green Door Tavern until it closed at midnight.

Which was about the time that Al Pardee, carrying his Beretta in his raincoat, decided that Drover wasn't coming back to the Drake Hotel any time soon and decided to take a cab back to his own hotel.

There would be time enough to kill Drover tomorrow.

THIRTY

MAE SAW the cab pull up to the canopy of the apartment building. The interior light flicked on and that was Homer reaching across the front seat with money in his hand.

And that was the other woman stepping onto the sidewalk.

Mae's hand was around the automatic in the pocket of her wet fur coat. The coat was slicked with rain, her hair was flat against her head, the deep red color turned almost black by rain.

Her eyes were dead now. The killer lights that had illuminated them as she stalked around the city that afternoon, burning off her excess hatred, were gone, replaced with this dead quality that was even more awful.

She stepped out of the shadow of the Northwestern University student union building on Lake Shore Drive and went down the steps. Cold and rain were nothing to her. The fur of the dead animals she wore around her rekindled the smell of the animals as they had been in life. This wasn't possible, of course; this was a good fur and the dead can't come back to life. She just was aware that she was cloaked in fur and was a dead animal herself.

He kissed her. Thirty feet away under a canopy. While Mae stood like a beast in the storm.

He slipped his arm around the black woman—Mae saw her clearly for a moment, saw the honey-brown face turned up toward Homer's in the light of the buildings's coach lamps—and then they started to part and then Mae was speaking to them. For a moment, neither they nor Mae knew that she was speaking. The voice came from the side of her brain and it was not her voice but it was using her throat and mouth to make its sound heard.

She stepped into the middle of the sidewalk. The cab lights winked away down the street.

She pulled the pistol clear. The barrel snagged on her pocket lining and she tore it clear.

The pistol was pointed the right way.

The man started to say something and he began by holding up his hand. Homer stared right at Mae and she wasn't even sure that he recognized her.

She fired.

There were nine rounds in the clip.

One.

Two.

Three.

Four.

Screams in the night. Lightning. Someone shouting behind her, ahead of her, inside her.

Five.

The woman in the red raincoat fell down on the sidewalk. Homer fell on top of her.

Six.

This was taking so damned long. It was like slow motion. It was a dream of falling. Fall and fall and never land.

Seven.

Eight.

Too many bullets.

Nine.

Click.

Click.

Click.

It was taking a moment to realize that she was out of bullets.

Shoved her hand in her pocket for the second clip. The dark metal slipped in her wet hand. Slapped it home with a click and pulled the recoil, seating the first round in the firing chamber.

Raised the pistol.

Homer was roaring at her. Let him roar, the dirty son of a bitch, pushing me down a hundred years ago, down on the car seat, so fucking sure of himself, doing it rough because that's the way a woman likes it, he said, and opening my legs and pulling down my panties and pushing his thing into me and up and down and up and down . . .

One.

Two.

The big body twitched up and he was coming after her. That made it easier.

Three.

Four.

Shouts and screams all around them.

Five.

An old man with a cane and a dog on a leash. The old man falling. Sorry old man, I didn't mean—

Six.

Shouts. Would they stop shouting?

Screaming? Stop screaming?

Seven.

And then she was on the pavement and someone was on top of her. The pistol clattered on the walk, skidding to the gutter, rain on her cheeks. Her coat would be ruined, rolling on the walk this way. . . .

THIRTY-ONE

THE FIRE department ambulance backed up to the emergency door at Northwestern Medical Center off Fairbanks Court at 2:13 A.M.

The stretchers were rolled into the room and banged through the doors to the operating theater. Helen Brown was already hooked up with IV lines. There was blood on her lips and nose and blood soaked the front of her white blouse and stained the left side of her tan trousers.

The second victim was the old man who had taken his elderly dog out for a walk on a rainy night; he had a bullet in his right lung. He was gasping in an oxygen mask and his signs were all bad.

The big man lumbered in after them. His coat was wet, splattered with rain and blood, and there was blood on the knuckles of his right hand where he had fallen on Helen.

It was such a mess.

THIRTY-TWO

Drover was in his own bed at the Drake at 8:30 in the morning. The fond memory of Ella Mackey of the night just past had floated into a dream. He was just getting to enjoy the dream when reality intruded like a knock. In fact, it was a knock.

The day was brilliant with sunlight. The night of rain had crept east, leaving no trace of itself except for the quality of the air. The bicyclists and runners were already going through their paces along the lakefront above Oak Street Beach.

The knock at the door said "Room service," but when Drover muttered "Go away," it insisted. Room service never insists in a classy hotel.

Drover opened his eyes. "Coming."

Drover pulled on his pants to open the door.

There were two of them, both in sports coats and shirts without ties. They had five-pointed metal stars to show him and he backed into the room. He pulled on the shirt he had worn the day before.

"My name is Morgan, this is O'Hare."

"Like the airport," Drover said.

"Like the airport," O'Hare said without enthusiasm. "Gee. I never thought of that before."

"What's up?"

"Do you know Homer White?"

"The baseball player."

O'Hare just waited in that cop's way that expresses mild irritation mixed with infinite patience. Neither policeman said anything.

"Yeah. What about him?"

"His ex-wife took a shot at him about six hours ago. Actually, she took a lot of shots at him," Morgan said.

"Shit," said Drover. It seemed most appropriate. He sat down hard on the straight chair by the desk. "Shit," he said again.

"What do you know about it?"

"What about Homer?"

"He's fine."

"You mean she missed?"

"Not exactly," Morgan said.

Drover frowned then. "Not exactly what exactly?"

"Were you working for Miss Tilson?"

"Who told you that?"

"She did."

"She's crazy."

"That may be too. What exactly brought you to Chicago?"

"Old home week. I grew up here."

"Here? In the Drake Hotel?"

"No. West Side."

"Oh," said Morgan as though that might mean something.

"What does not exactly mean?" Drover said.

"I beg your pardon?" O'Hare said.

"Did she shoot someone or just try to shoot someone?"

"Who would she have wanted to shoot?"

Drover saw the way it was going to be. He looked down at his hands folded across his knees. Then looked at the two cops. One sat in the other chair. The second was circling the room, looking at things.

"Well?" said O'Hare.

"Why don't we cut the Mickey Mouse?" Drover said.

It was the wrong thing to say.

An hour later, he was sitting in a windowless room at Area Six Homicide on the North Side of the city. They had taken his cuffs off and told him to stay where he was. He sat in the room and waited for them to come back. It was going to be a long morning.

They let him go at one in the afternoon. The bright day was still bright.

They put him in a lineup around noon with a couple of other guys, including two cops who looked nothing like him. Mae identified him right away. But, curiously, this had led to no official action.

He finally guessed they thought Mae Tilson was cracked. Or maybe they had talked to Homer again and he had put the right spin on it this time and explained that Drover had flown to Chicago to save Homer, not to get him killed.

Mae Tilson had fired sixteen nine-millimeter rounds at various targets on North Lake Shore Drive at 1:12 A.M. She had struck Miss Helen Brown of 1545 North LaSalle Street three times. She had shot and killed Herbert C. Rosewood, eighty-one, of 124 East Chestnut Street, with a single shot to the chest. The rest of her shots went wild. She was being held for observation at Cook County Hospital and, preliminarily, had been charged with various counts, including murder and attempted murder.

Homer White had involved Drover in this about six in the morning.

In separate questioning, the police mentioned Drover's name to Mae Tilson and she had reacted. *Reacted* was the favorite word of Detective O'Hare. In fact, she began bouncing off the walls then, babbling on and on about someone named Max Heubner and about Drover and about Eddie Briggs of the Cubs and how Drover had tried to seduce her one night in Seattle. . . .

Drover left Area Six headquarters with a strong sense of failure.

Drover called Kelly when he got back to the hotel. Kelly was his pet rock when he needed to hang on to something.

Kelly told him to come home to California.

He said he couldn't.

Kelly then said to hold tight. The rock would come to the prophet. Or something like that.

Drover didn't say no. When you need a friend, you need a friend.

THIRTY-THREE

HOMER WHITE and Mrs. E. L. Brown shared the otherwise empty visitors' lounge on the third floor. The nurses' station was a bright island in the middle of the long corridor. The hospital is among the best in the world but people still die in it.

That's where Drover found them shortly before 6:00 P.M.

Helen's mother was smaller than Helen and her fingers said her life had been harder. They were worn around the knuckles.

Drover came into the lounge and sat down without speaking.

Homer looked at him and then looked away.

Drover stared at Homer and then at Mrs. Brown.

"My name is Drover. I met your daughter yesterday."

Mrs. Brown gave him the look. It spoke for what she didn't say.

"Homer, you gave my name to the cops. That's twice now, counting ten years ago. You have this thing for people in authority."

"Aw, man. Go fuck yourself, I can't think about you or talk to you right now."

"How's Helen?" he said.

"How you think she is? She was shot, man, what the hell do you think about that? And you said you talked to Mae in Seattle and all I know, you got that crazy bitch to come down here and do what she did."

Mrs. Brown said nothing. She looked from one white man to the other and didn't say a thing.

"I talked to the cops a good part of the day. They think Mae is crazy. They don't like it because they would like to fry her but they think she might be crazy."

"She is crazy. Why would she do this to Helen? To me?"

"Because you wanted to marry Helen."

Mrs. Brown held still, looking from one boy to the other. That was her daughter somewhere in the depth of this building with tubes in her nose and in her arms and blood dripping down into her. She contained herself.

"Goddamnit, if she wanted all my money, I would of given her the farm, everything she wanted, she didn't have to do this."

"People get crazy," Drover said.

"You lie," Mrs. Brown said. Not to Drover. She was looking at Homer White. "My daughter never marry white trash like you. You may think she marry you but she never would."

"Miz Brown, I was a-courting her. She made me walk when I thought I couldn't walk, she—"

"She was doin' what she does, she wasn' doin' nothin' she wouldn't do for anyone else," Mrs. Brown said. "You sorry white trash, why you involve my daughter in your sorry white-trash life—" She stopped, not because words failed her but because her despair overwhelmed her. Her eyes were wet. "Police asking questions. Police all around here. You got yourself a wife and your wife carries around a piece and is gonna shoot you and shoots my Helen. What kind of sorry trash you brought to her? To me? Nothing but grief, white-trash grief. She is so much above you, you can't even see her."

Homer White said nothing then. He looked at the woman in her anger and couldn't find a word.

And neither could Drover.

They just sat there and looked at each other or, more often, looked away.

THIRTY-FOUR

Dover left the hospital at 8:00 P.M. A doctor came into the visitors' lounge and spoke to them about Helen Brown in that distracted way of doctors who do not want to get themselves involved in the reactions of nonpatients. The essence of his grave words was that her condition was much better and that she would have a restful night and there was no reason to wait around to see her because she had been sedated.

He was telling everyone to go home.

After he left, Homer started to speak with Mrs. Brown again and Drover thought he had seen enough of that. He slipped on his raincoat and didn't bother to say good-bye to anyone.

On the way to the elevator, he stopped at a water fountain and drank deeply. When he got to the elevator bank, Homer was there as well. They didn't bother to speak to each other.

Homer White and Drover left the building at the same time. But not together.

The night was full of spring. It was warm and the breeze smelled faintly perfumed by the buds suddenly growing along bare branches in the parks.

Drover was tired but he was too awake to head back to the hotel. Besides, Kelly was supposed to be flying in around ten. Maybe he'd kill an hour just walking on the lakefront.

He took the underground passage beneath Lake Shore Drive to the lakefront.

The rocks that formed the seawall were square building blocks, each weighing a few tons, forming a passable pathway between the highway and the lake waters. The moon was full and bright on the waters. He walked north around the curve toward the Oak Street Beach. He wasn't thinking of any one thing. Or maybe he was mostly thinking about Helen Brown getting the punishment Homer deserved.

If anyone really deserves what they get in the end.

He was chilled by the time he reached the beach and decided to call it a walk. He took the tunnel under the drive to the back entrance of the Drake Hotel and went inside.

He stopped at the Coq d'Or bar before going upstairs. He ordered a Red Label on the rocks and nursed it, watching snatches of the White Sox game on the television. He tried to get into it but then he realized no one in the room was into it. It was just on and it was a bar and American culture demanded that every bar have a TV set on all the time. He could remember when that wasn't true in a classy place like the Coq d'Or. But then, he could remember when you got salted peanuts in a bar instead of trail mix.

"Hello, funny man."

The voice was right next to him.

He started to turn but a finger prodded him hard in the kidney.

And he just knew it wasn't a finger at all.

He stared straight ahead at the red-jacketed barman working on drinks at the other end.

"You remember me, funny guy?"

"You were the guy in the hat. In the car with Leonardo. In Seattle. You called me 'funny guy' then too."

"The guy in the hat. Yeah. The guy in the hat." He said it as though it might be the punchline to a joke. "We gave you some material that night. I didn't read all about it in any newspaper like I was expecting to do."

"Yeah. Well, newspapers are funny that way. They usually want the news to have an element of truth to it, even in the sports pages."

"You didn't think it was true?"

"Xeroxes of betting slips supposedly initialed by Homer White. Along with an incriminating eight-by-ten glossy of Homer sitting at a booth with the illustrious Mafia boss Tony Ricci and a not very illustrious fat man."

"The picture was proof."

"The picture was a setup, a paste job. But very flattering to you, I must say."

"You still think this is a joke, funny guy?"

"That's a gun, isn't it?"

The fat man probed the kidney again and Drover squinted in pain.

"You're so smart, Drover, you just outsmarted yourself."

"Is that a gun in my back or are you pretending?" Drover said it easily but there was a line of sweat breaking out above his upper lip. He wiped his hand across his mouth. His tongue was dry. All kinds of little things showed just how nervous he was.

"A nine-millimeter Beretta. With a silencer so that when I shoot it off in my pocket, it won't make hardly no sound at all."

"Some reason we can't be friends?" Drover tried. Damn. Now his hand was trembling. He pressed it down hard on the copper bar top.

"You still don't know who I am, do you?"

"The guy in the hat in the car in Seattle. The guy in the photograph with Ricci and Homer White."

"Al Pardee."

Drover blinked.

"You remember now?"

"What am I supposed to remember?"

"You fucking prick, you sent me over."

"I sent you over what?"

"Keep fucking around with me, I'll open up your back right here and now, I swear I will—"

"I don't know who you are. I don't know any Al Pardee."

"Ten years ago. When you were indicted. In L.A. And then you walked and I did the time. Three years."

"What do you mean?"

Al Pardee said, "Turn around and look at me."

The pressure against his back lessened. Drover turned and looked at the fat man. He searched the piggy eyes for some sense and didn't see any.

"Ten years ago," Drover said. He kept it low. "I was indicted by a hotdog D.A. in Los Angeles who wanted to pretty up his package of known figures going down on RICO charges. I was window dressing. My voice was on ten seconds of tape in a public place with a known figure named Ziggy Weisel. Ziggy was a gambler. I knew him. I knew him from the old neighborhood. End of connection. When it came to trial, my indictment was lost because there wasn't anything to it in the first place."

"Bullshit. You gave them me. You were wired or something. I saw you around the fringes of the action but I didn't really have dealings with you. But the prosecutor, that guy Jennings, he said you had a deal and that I was named by you—"

"Al. Al, can I get your attention a minute? I don't know you, Al, I don't know who you are, the first time I ever saw you was in that car with Leonardo in Seattle—"

"I did three years, and when I got out it was a tough parole. And you were walking around free all that time. I knew I'd get you some- time, I knew it. I put you in my files. I knew you were living in Santa Cruz, I knew you worked for that geek in Vegas, Vernon, but I had to wait to use you. And then you investigated Homer White for gam- bling last winter and Mr. Heubner knew about it and he wanted to know more, he wanted to see if he could bring Homer to Seattle. It was a good time for me to get involved with you but you fucked it up, you didn't use the picture I gave you—"

"What would you have done if I used the picture?"

"What do you think? I was going to have you whacked. But now my friend in Chicago is backing out on it, you put some pressure on Sal Marconi in Vegas, on Elmore—you are one tough prick to get killed."

Drover let his eyes wander the paneled room with its soft lights and murmurs of conversation. Just a nice, civilized little public place where a guy in a raincoat had a pistol and was talking about his frustrations with trying to get Drover murdered. Poor Al Pardee. Drover would have said that out loud if his mouth hadn't been so dry.

"I was disappointed you didn't recognize me that night in Seattle. I put on about a hundred pounds over the last ten years. I suppose that's why."

"You should go on a diet. Get some exercise."

"Funny guy. You got a mouth on you, you might as well use it while it still works."

"What are you gonna do?"

"What do you think, funny guy? We're going up to your room. I been waiting around for you for two days. We're gonna talk a little and then we're gonna stop talking. If you don't like that, I can whack you here and now. You think any of these geeks is gonna stop me?"

"Al, look, you want me to use the picture of Homer, I'll use it. I'll place it—"

"Fuck you, smart guy. We're going up to the room and get the picture and then we're gonna settle this."

"You're carrying the wrong grudge, Al. I don't know you, I never knew you, I don't give a shit what some prosecutor told you. That's lawyers' humor. I don't put stock in it."

"Then the joke's on you," Al Pardee said.

Drover dropped a twenty-dollar bill on his tab and turned from the bar. Always leave a good tip, especially if it's your last.

Not that he believed that.

He would go down swinging. But not here. There wasn't any room to maneuver. Al Pardee was right next to him and at this distance, Al couldn't miss.

They left the café by the side door and went down a marbled hall to the elevator bank.

The doors pinged open and a lady in uniform stood at the buttons. Drover mentioned his floor number and the doors closed. The two men stood side by side. Drover thought Al was loosening up just a little bit. On the other hand, Drover thought of all the movies he had seen in which the hero suddenly shoves the bad guy with the gun and jumps to the side or over the cliff or out the window and prevails. This wasn't at all like a movie.

The two men got off the elevator at the sixth floor.

They walked down the quiet corridor to the room at the end. Drover slapped his pockets and shook his head. "I don't have my entrance card. I must have left it in the room."

"That's a shame," Al Pardee said. "Then I'll have to whack you right here and now."

"No, wait. I've found it."

He opened the door to the room. The bed was made. He walked to the leather chair by the desk and turned.

"Siddown," Al Pardee said.

He didn't want to sit down. Heroes don't sit down when they're about to get the jump on a bad guy.

"I said sit," Al Pardee said.

Drover sat. Hands on knees. Staring at the big man who pulled a big pistol from his raincoat pocket. It was muzzled with a silencer that made it look that much bigger.

"I'm gonna tell you something," Drover said. "I really, honestly, truly don't know who you are or what this is about."

"Cross your heart and hope to die?"

"Honest to God."

"God, I like the way you look right now. The way I wanted you to look all those nights inside when I thought about getting you. You look like you're gonna puke. Guys do that sometimes when they're gonna get it and they know it, sometimes they puke."

"All right, Al. Just tell me this, what does all this have to do with Homer White?"

"Homer White? I don't give a shit about Homer White. This is nothing about Homer White. Heubner wanted to get Homer banned from baseball for some reason. I think he wanted to whack Homer but you can't just whack a major league baseball star, you got to get the guy out of his environment. I think he wanted to whack him in Arkansas but then Homer didn't want to go back to Arkansas again, he met some girl in Chicago he liked, and whatever it was, it was a typical Heubner deal, all complicated maneuvers to get some property belongs to this rube."

"Jesus. His ex-wife just tried to kill Homer not twenty hours ago."

"Mae? Mae Tilson? Here in Chicago?"

"Yeah, Al. And the cops are hustling on this one. They came for me this morning, talked to me, came right to this hotel room. They said they're coming back."

Drover watched the reaction. It was a good one, in slow time, and for a moment, Al Pardee turned and looked at the door.

Drover tried to do it the way John Wayne would have done it. He did get one hand on the barrel and stuck a finger from the other hand in Pardee's little eye.

Pardee bellowed, stepped back, and slapped the pistol down hard on Drover's left shoulder.

Drover dropped to one knee because of the lightning bolt of pain that connected the shoulder with his broken head and busted ribs.

Al Pardee hit him again with the pistol, bringing it down savagely across his face, breaking his nose. Blood welled at Drover's nostrils.

"You like that, hero? You like that?" Pardee was saying it between his clenched teeth.

Drover wiped at the blood on his lips.

"You like that, hero?" Pardee said inanely again and swung the pistol again and struck the side of Drover's head so that the bells started ringing in the ear canals.

"Jesus," Drover groaned.

Al's gun hand trembled.

"Al, you're gonna take a fall on this, on sending Mae to Chicago to kill Homer White and his girlfriend. You and your boss, Heubner—"

Al Pardee grinned then. "You still don't get it, you dumb shit. I don't work for Heubner. I mean, he thinks I work for him but I work for Mr. Frank Chesrow—"

Drover gaped then. "You work for the U.S attorney? You're an undercover snitch for them, is that it?"

Al Pardee said, "I do what I gotta—"

"A snitch! You're a low-life snitch and that's what you accuse me of doing to you ten years ago. Only you're doing it right here and now and it's beginning to look like murder. You put the U.S. attorney on to me. And my girlfriend. You probably were the one to bring me in on this in the first place, you dumb bastard."

"Frank Chesrow thinks I'm in L.A. I'll be in L.A. when they put you in a box."

Drover tried to think through the pain. He didn't want to accept it. The pain would end in a few moments and so would his life.

"Al, I can get you money—"

"I don't need no money, you asshole. Not from you."

And he fired.

The bullet thudded into the fleshy part of the thigh of Drover's left leg. The force of the round threw him back on the stained rug.

He was shot.

Drover blinked and realized it and looked down at the wound.

For a moment, there was nothing but adrenaline muffling the pain.

Then the hurt began, a warm, spreading pain that moved down to his knee and up to his groin and the underside of his belly. The stain on his trousers was very dark and he knew it was blood.

"You shot me, Al," he said in the distant, shocked way some soldiers speak of their wounds on battlefields.

"Yeah. I told you I was gonna whack you and now I started doing it. You want the next one in your mouth?"

"Jesus, Al. This really hurts."

"It's supposed to hurt."

Drover felt like throwing up because of the pain in his leg. He tried it on the rug. The pain didn't get better and now his stomach ached as well.

"It really hurts, don't it?" Pardee said.

"It really hurts."

"I thought every day about taking you out, but the timing was always wrong," Al Pardee rattled on. "Can't do a hit in Vegas because that's protected territory. I could of hit you in Santa Cruz but you were always around people like that fireman buddy of yours or that barmaid. Always around people."

"You could of hit me in Seattle a week ago."

"Naw. I wanted to set you up, do some work for me so I get in better with Heubner and that helps me out with my real boss, Frank

Chesrow. See? But you didn't do what you were supposed to do, so now I don't wanna wait no more. I'm just gonna whack you—"

"And Ricci? In Chicago? He'll know it was you, Al. That isn't very smart."

"What would Ricci do? Tell the cops?"

"He might tell someone else, someone who wouldn't want me killed," Drover said then. His voice was dull because of the effort of talking above the pain.

"Like who?"

"Like Tony Rolls. I marked you this time, Al. You should just scuttle back to Seattle like the three-legged alligator you are and forget any thought of whacking anybody," Drover said. He grimaced because it was all hurting, all the words. "You wanna know why Ricci doesn't want to do a hit for you? Because Tony Rolls told him you were working for the U.S. attorney."

"You're lying. You didn't know until this moment I was working for Frank Chesrow, you lying bastard," Al Pardee said.

"I got friends," Drover went on. "Tony Rolls is one."

"Tony Rolls is out of the trade," Al Pardee said.

"No one is ever retired," Drover said.

"Well, that's a chance I have to take."

They stared at each other.

"Say good night, Gracie," Al Pardee said. He pointed the muzzle at Drover's forehead.

The door smashed open.

Al Pardee turned and Drover made another dive toward him.

But it wasn't necessary.

Black Kelly came through the opening door low, like a center on the offensive line after the snap. He was rising but rising under the hand that held the pistol.

Pardee fired as Drover hit him from behind.

The silencer went whump.

The round shattered plaster above the doorway. Kelly's huge head smashed into Pardee's belly at the same time.

Drover grabbed for the pistol.

It was Pardee's turn to go whump.

Kelly landed on Pardee belly to belly, the weight of a lineman on a tub of lard. They were both testimonies to the building blocks of the body formed by countless racks of barbecued ribs. At the bottom of the football pile was Drover, still struggling for the pistol.

Kelly noticed the struggle and intervened with a sudden grip that snapped Pardee's wrist. The gun fell silently to the rug and Pardee thought to scream. And did.

Drover pushed at the pile of bodies on top of him.

Pardee screamed again.

Drover whispered, "Get off me, Kelly, you guys weigh a quarter ton easy."

"The thanks I get," Kelly said, struggling up. He grabbed Pardee by the collar and shoved his bulk onto the bed. Drover picked up the pistol from the floor and pointed it at Pardee.

"You fucking bastard," Pardee said.

"Kelly," Drover began but stopped. Words took too much effort and he was finding it hard to breathe.

Kelly grabbed the pistol out of his weak hand. "Go over to the phone and dial nine-one-one for a fire department ambulance," Kelly said.

"Why? Who needs an ambulance." Drover suddenly felt like lying down and taking a long rest. He staggered to the desk and fell into the chair. He reached for the phone. It all took a very long time and there was all this pain involved with every act.

The cops came as the fire department paramedics were wheeling Drover out of the room on a stretcher. Kelly explained some of it to the cops then and the rest came out after Drover was X-rayed, operated on, and bandaged in the same hospital complex where Helen Brown also spent a sedated night. Al Pardee was treated for a broken wrist at Cook County Hospital before going to Area Six police headquarters on the North Side. All the while, Al kept babbling about his boss, Frank Chesrow, and offering the cops many phone numbers.

The Chicago cops found it all fascinating. Especially when they placed long-distance calls to Seattle.

At one in the morning, Drover awoke in the hospital bed to find out he was not dead. This surprised him for a moment. Then he heard the familiar rumble of Black Kelly's voice in the darkness. Then he saw the form looming over the bed.

"How ya doin', kid?"

"I'm better than I feel, I think," Drover said.

"Aren't you glad I decided to come out to Chicago to see you?"

"Your timing was good," Drover said.

"Actually, it was bad. The plane was delayed an hour getting into O'Hare. When I got to the hotel, I thought you might be in the bar. No particular reason but I went in the joint and asked about you and the barman said you were there and left with this other guy. I asked him what the other guy looked like and he told me. Your Seattle buddy."

"I'm amazed he remembered anything," Drover said.

"Well, he said you left him a fifteen-dollar tip on a five-dollar drink. It always pays to leave a good tip," Kelly said.

"I'll remember that," Drover said.

"Get some sleep, pal," Kelly said.

"I owe you again."

"I know. I'm keeping score," Kelly said.

THIRTY-FIVE

HELEN BROWN left the hospital ten days later. Her mother allowed Homer White to drive her home. Her mother had cleaned the apartment three times, washed every dish twice, and put vases of flowers everywhere. There were flowers from people Helen Brown didn't even know and some she knew not very well. There was a big comic card from the staff at the rehabilitation institute and everyone had signed their names.

Homer White had been traded to the Kansas City Royals in the American League the previous Wednesday. They had written him a new contract, full of incentives and potentially worth more than his Cubs contract. If he didn't get an attack of old age and fail as a designated hitter.

The Cubs got one long reliever with a good track record and a draft choice. Everyone in baseball thought the Cubs had cut a pretty good deal. It all depended on what Homer White did in Kansas City.

His new manager had given him the day off to fly to Chicago to take Helen Brown out of the hospital.

The third of May. Definite buds in the trees. Definite greening of the grass in Lincoln Park. The sun was flexing muscles up and down the lakefront and a few of the joggers were shirtless. A man threw a stick for a dog on the sand. A girl sunbathed on her towel. Two homeless men sat in the chess pavilion and stared at the world marching by.

Homer was very protective. He might have been bringing a new mother home from the hospital. He helped her into the building and sort of hovered over her. He had earned a couple of smiles from her and they were reward enough.

They entered the apartment with her key.

Her mother was waiting in the kitchen, smiling at her, and Helen was required to walk around and smell the flowers. There were flowers in every room. It was very touching and she was easily touched.

She had thought about that during ten days and nights in a hospital bed.

About Homer and what he wanted.

And about things as they were.

They ate a small meal because that's all Helen wanted. She had lost weight and she didn't need to. Her cheeks were sunken but her eyes were bright.

She told her mother in the bedroom that she wanted to speak to Homer alone. Her mother made a face but she left in a little while.

They were together and they weren't.

He felt it more than anything said.

He wanted to kiss her and he didn't.

She came into the living room and sat down. There was still a little pain and her joints felt stiff. She sat on the old-fashioned high armchair that had belonged to her grandmother. It was the most comfortable and beautiful chair in the room.

Homer sat down on the couch.

It was just 7:00 P.M.

"I got the last flight out back to Kansas City and the first flight in the morning," Homer finally said.

She understood.

She looked out the window at the bright ribbon on empty LaSalle Street.

"Honey, I don't ever want to hurt you."

"And I don't ever want to hurt you, Homer."

When she looked back at him, she said, "I thought I might fall in love with you deep. The way you thought you felt about me. And I did, finally. I think I did. I can't measure it in me any more than I can measure it in you. It was all right. But we can't escape things. We really can't, Homer."

"Sure we can, Honey, we can escape. You just try and try and never give up. I never expected to see Eddie Briggs give me a new lease on life. DH in KC. It's a good team, we can win the pennant. Not next year but this year."

"Good. I know you can do your best. You've found yourself—"

"My legs, it's amazing when you ain't standin' around three hours a day how much difference it makes—"

"Homer—"

"Don't, Honey, I can't stand it. You wanna say something to me and I can't take it. Take a little time, think it out. I know it'll be hard but it won't be the hardest thing ever was done. There's lots of white and black people married to each other. City like this, it don't matter. We got our lives, I don' care if I was never to go back to Caswell again. My old life is over, this is my new life."

She waited. She didn't want to smile at him because that would have encouraged him.

His eyes looked lost, she thought.

"I'm not going to marry you," she said.

"Because of Mae? I beg you to forgive me, I'll beg you every day of my life, Honey, honest to God, I'll make it up to you."

"No. I don't want you to beg, Homer. What that woman did was in her own mind, it wasn't that. I wouldn't have married you if that had happened or didn't happen. I'm not talking about that. Or about her. It's just you and me, Homer."

"You and me is pretty good, Honey."

"We're terrible," she said.

He blinked at her.

"I felt sorry for you, Homer. That isn't love. And you finally met someone who might bring out the best in you. The stuff you always had anyway. The courage. You just let it get covered up with a lot of other things. The thing you did well was baseball, so you thought that was the only thing that mattered."

"And you changed that in me."

"You changed yourself."

"No. It was you, Honey, not me."

"I'm sorry, Homer. I can't love you."

"Why?"

"I don't know."

"Hell, Honey. We're both not gettin' younger. I got a growed daughter. Why don't we just make each other happy? I mean, we don't have to get married. You got your place, I got mine. I'll just come to see you, take you out for walks on the lakefront, take you to Greektown. Hell, I'd eat French food to be with you."

Damnit.

She smiled, and she was specifically not going to smile.

"Escargots," he said. "Eat that fish in milk sauce. Anything."

Still smiling.

He went down on one knee and reached out his hands for hers. He had very large hands, roughened by nineteen seasons in the Bigs, and his wrists were knotted with solid layers of muscle. His hands were browned by sun and hers by God.

"All right, Homeboy," she said. "No promises. No pleading."

"I won't even get down on my knees again," he said.

"My mother really doesn't approve at all."

"I know, I know, she made that pretty clear to me over the past ten days," Homer said.

"So you're not in that part of my life," she said. "And I might meet someone and fall in love and break your heart."

He nodded his head up and down. "I know, I know, chance I take."

"And you should see girls."

"I seen girls, Honey, but you're a woman."

"I mean it. This isn't going anywhere, Homeboy."

"I know it, Lord, I know it. But I'm sellin' the farm anyway now that I know about that development and why Mae wanted it so bad. Poor ol' Mae is cracked up and I'm gonna see to her as well. And Millie, take care of Millie. Then buy me that condo I been rentin' and sit there in the winter and watch the lake freeze."

"This isn't going anywhere, you know," she said, still with her hands in his.

"I know, I know," he promised, lying like he always did.

THIRTY-SIX

O<small>N THE</small> fourth of July, there were fireworks above the water in Santa Cruz. Some of the hippies who lounged around the town all year and acted sour to kids didn't like that. It was too damned patriotic and they were still fighting against the Vietnam War. They were gray-haired hippies now, with pot bellies and flowered shirts, who smoked dope on the beach and cursed the pigs. No celebration in Santa Cruz was complete without them.

The fireworks spun up in the night sky, whirled, opened into umbrellas of light and fell to the sea. Everyone went *oh* and *ah* on cue. It only lasted twenty minutes but it was terrific, just terrific.

And afterward, they all went back into Kelly's place and sat around the big round table in the corner that was the owner's private preserve. They ate the evening meal together. Kelly and Drover called it supper, Lori and Nancy called it dinner, and Neil O'Neill had called in missing because he was doing the play-by-play on the Kansas City Royals–Chicago White Sox game on ESPN. Neil was part of the extended family that had priority access to the round table in the back whenever the family met.

They watched the game on one of the sets. The Royals threw blanks at the White Sox for seven innings and Homer White, the DH, went two for three. He was now hitting .278 and his incentives were kicking in almost every week. A DH with twenty-one homers in mid-season is nothing to sneeze at.

Neither was the record of the long reliever the Cubs picked up from KC. His earned-run average was just above two.

Everybody was happy, right?

"What do you think it means when Homer White sends me a check for ten thousand dollars?" Drover asked. It was just dropped into the conversation at the seventh-inning stretch.

Kelly stared at him.

Drover smiled back. He was finally off crutches and had graduated to a cane and a slight twinge at the hip that came from walking funny for two months.

"It means he sold his farm," Kelly said.

"That was nice," Lori said.

"But what does it mean?" Drover said.

Kelly snapped his red suspenders. Sometimes he overdid the fire-house thing but he was too nice a guy to tell that to. He was even talking about buying a Dalmatian puppy, for Pete's sake. "Sometimes, as Freud said once, ten thousand dollars is just ten thousand dollars."

"That was a cigar," Lori said. She could be too literal-minded but no one would tell her because she was sweet as well.

"Maybe it's going well with Helen," Nancy said.

They looked at her.

"Like passing out cigars when your wife has a baby," Nancy persisted.

"Was there a note?"

"Nope. Just a certified check. I doubt that Homer can write anyway," Drover said.

"Come on. The guy didn't turn out to be that bad," Lori said. She was a person who could be counted on to stick up for people she didn't know. If you bad-mouthed someone, you were probably over-doing it, in Lori's book.

"Nobody did. Except for Pardee. He blew the cover on the Heubner case and the G doesn't need him anymore. He violated his parole shooting me. And he's getting hit with attempted homicide in Chicago if the G lets him go. He's going to be in prison." Drover shook his head. "And all over something that he got wrong."

"From now on, we ought to forget the past," Lori said.

"You mean, just repeat it?" Drover said.

"I mean, let's get off the pier and go up in the hills and find that roadhouse and dance all night. I'm tired of this stupid baseball game," she said.

They sat there a moment looking at each other and then at her.

"I can't dance with a cane," Drover said.

"You can't dance without one," Lori said.

"Go get him, honey," Nancy said.

Drover held up his hands. "I quit. *No mas.*"

"What do you say?"

They piled in Kelly's bus and headed up into the hills, leaving behind the national pastime on network television. They were all tired of this stupid baseball game.

AFTERWORD

THE KANSAS City Royals finished second, two games behind the Oakland As.

The Cubs finished fourth.

Al Pardee went back to prison.

The case against Max Heubner resulted in a thirty-one-count indictment on RICO charges. It awaits trial.

Mae Tilson was judged not guilty by reason of insanity. She is still a patient at Elgin State Mental Health Center.

Lori Gibbons took the LSAT test in the fall and is looking forward to her new career as a law student.

Homer White did not sell the farm. The real estate market remained depressed.

He and Helen Brown got married after the season anyway and they are alive and well in Chicago. In the off season.